O.M.: The Indian Science Fiction Anthology

Volume 1: COVID-19

Compiled & Edited by

RISHABH DUBEY 'KRIDIOUS'

Ukiyoto Publishing

All global publishing rights are held by

Ukiyoto Publishing

Published in 2024

ISBN

9789360499990

www.ukiyoto.com

THE O.M. PROJECT

ॐ (Om) symbolizes the Universe and the ultimate reality. It is one of the most important symbols of Indian history. Per belief, at the dawn of creation, from emptiness, first emerged a syllable consisting of three letters – A-U-M (often written as OM).

Emanated at the very beginning of the universe, or the *Brahmaan*, the reverberating sound of Om has been reimagined into the Latin acronym- O.M.: standing for **Oculus Magnus**, or *The Great Eye* or *The Big Eye*; representing the all-seeing eye of yesterday, today and tomorrow, something befitting for Indian Science Fiction.

O.M.: The Indian Science Fiction Anthology, is an aspirational project, which aims to bring out the essence and diversity of Indian Science Fiction to Global Platforms annually. This Volume, with the subject of the COVID-19 pandemic, is the pilot publication of the project. With globally significant and relevant themes, the O.M. project will release at least one anthology each year, starting in 2024.

Featured Authors

Archana Mirajkar

Arvind Mishra

Charu Thapliyal

Debraj Moulick

K S Purushothaman

Kshama Gautam

Nilesh Malvankar

Pragya Gautam

Rishabh Dubey 'Kridious'

Sapna Katti

Seema Kulkarni

Smita Potnis

Soham Guha

Sourav Ghosh

Subha Das Mollick

Varun Sayal

Contents

Introduction to the Stories

i. **A Scientist's Clairvoyance:** *Seema Kulkarni* explores a Uchronia in her story, whereby the entire series of events leading to the pandemic, and the ones that followed have all been reimagined.

ii. **ACE+:** *K. S. Purushothaman* writes his rendition of a post-corona and post-lockdown time, known as the 'After the Corona Era' or 'ACE', where he narrates the impact of the same on humankind and the world.

iii. **Aftermath:** A world eight years beyond its recovery from the pandemic is depicted in this futuristic story by *Soham Guha.*

iv. **An Indian's Blood:** *Subha Das Mollick* narrates fictional accounts of events that unfolded after the pandemic, contrasting the cities of New York and Kolkata.

v. **Humanity Triumphs:** In her story, *Smita Potnis* talks about an era 30 years after the pandemic and how the world has slowly learned to adapt to it.

vi. **Mazdur Dhaba:** *Saurav Ghosh*, in his story, portrays the financial repercussions and struggles, especially of the lower economic classes, as a result of the pandemic and its aftermath.

vii. **Mind over Matter:** In this story, *Archana Mirajkar* has explored the possibilities concerning an absolute cure against a virus that is novel in all its attributes.

viii. **NOSTOS:** *Debraj Moulick*, in his story, depicts an account of the sudden and necessary transition of the city that never slept, that is Mumbai, to an isolated town with empty streets, all given to the pandemic.

ix. **Seeds of Hope:** *Varun Sayal* tells a fictional account of a small family, living in a lockdown-struck world in the pandemic.

x. **Shortcoming:** The story by *Nilesh Malvankar* narrates a fictional account of finding a cure for the coronavirus which results in a not-so-favourable side-effect.

xi. **The Deal:** The short fiction by *Pragya Gautam* incorporates and builds on the idea of special viral proteins and presents a dark reality through the lens of a questionable protagonist.

xii. **The Earths of our Past:** This Space Sci-Fi by *Charu Thapliyal* explores the possibilities of higher-dimensional existence made possible as an indirect impact of the pandemic.

xiii. **The Last Hope:** In his story, *Rishabh Dubey 'Kridious'* goes on a massive hunt to find individuals with natural antibodies that could be administered in people still not affected by the pandemic.

xiv. **The Proof:** *Sapana Katti* dwells in post-pandemic in-depth research on the subject of coronavirus in her futuristic story.

xv. **Unheard Screams:** *Kshama Gautam* writes a fictional account highlighting the plight of isolated students in lockdown as well as the paranoia resulting from the pandemic.

xvi. **Homecoming:** *Dr Arvind Mishra* recalls the whole journey of the Pandemic in this story; leveraging the pen of brevity with the ink of Science Fiction.

KOVID KAVITA

KOVID KAVITA

-Rishabh Dubey 'Kridious'

Our Nation was submerged in a dark gloom,
But how did it all come to this?
Was it a testament to our impending doom?
Or THE PROOF of our apocalypse?

The SHORTCOMING lay in our ignorance,
When it first entered AN INDIAN's BLOOD;
We should've shown more vigilance,
And worked to just nip it in the bud.

Unseen even in the worst of our dreams,
The plight of those left alone;
The desperate yet UNHEARD SCREAMS,
Of the MAZDUR returning home.

And also, the resonating screams of those
Gathering knowledge or wealth in foreign terrains;
Whose screams appear strangely a bit close
For the same HOMECOMING to their native plains.

But we knew that we would outlast.
We just had to entirely embrace,
The NOSTOS of THE EARTHS OF OUR PAST,
That narrated the coming of an ACE.

The pandemic taught us all,
The might of MIND OVER MATTER;
In the end, the mind stands tall,
And just illusions define the latter.

There are still SEEDS OF HOPE,
In the SCIENTISTS' CLAIRVOYANCE;
Perhaps, in them, is THE LAST HOPE,
To make sure HUMANITY TRIUMPHS.

THE DEAL is to not just survive,
But intercept the apocalypse in its path,
To find a way to sustain and thrive
And be ready to face the AFTERMATH.

A SCIENTIST'S
CLAIRVOYANCE

A SCIENTIST'S CLAIRVOYANCE

-Seema Kulkarni

Seema Kulkarni hails from Dharwad in Karnataka. Her educational qualifications include M.Sc., M.Phil. in Solid state Physics and a diploma in French from Karnataka University, Dharwad. Presently she is working as the volunteer coordinator in one of the Myanmar Refugees Community Learning Centres under the protection of UNHCR in Kuala Lumpur, Malaysia. Seema has been a freelance journalist for Gulf News, UAE. Seema has released two poetry collections in Kannada, the second one is a joint collection with her mother. Her two SF stories were presented at the SF Conference 2020 and 2021, organized by IASFS and are a part of the SF story collections published by University Publications. Seema's science articles, short stories, articles, essays, translated Southeast Asian folk stories for children and poems have been published in popular Kannada magazines, newspapers and web magazines. Seema has won state-level awards in poetry and short story competitions.

The following story is not a story of India with which we are acquainted with. But it narrates the story of an alternate history of India, which had a diverted course of actions to fight the COVID-19 pandemic than what we are familiar with …a different scenario, different scientists, and even the Prime Minister. So, let us start the story…

June 2010 – July 2011

"The single biggest threat to man's continued dominance on the planet is the virus."

Anyone visiting Dr Medha Bhargav and Dr Samyak Bhargav's laboratory set up at the Indian Centre of Virology Research (ICVR) in Bengaluru (Bangalore) would never fail to notice this quote by Nobel laureate Joshua Lederberg, displayed on an LED screen mounted on the wall, facing the entrance. ICVR has been designated as one of the collaborating laboratories of the World Health Organization (WHO).

The husband and wife undoubtedly have been among the most respected virologists not only in India but also all over the world in the past two decades for their pioneering work in the field. Dr Medha and Dr Samyak Bhargav are recipients of the 'India Science Award'- the highest and the most prestigious national-level recognition by the Government of India for excellence in science. They are among the twelve nominated members to an advisory body to the Government of India - 'India Epidemics Advisory Committee' (IEAC). IEAC advises the government on strengthening the country's defences against infectious diseases through research and development strategies to fight epidemics using Artificial

Intelligence (AI) besides developing vaccinations against Emerging Infectious Diseases (EID). Bhargavs are also honorary members of several renowned international virology research institutes and networks that are coalitions such as the Global Virus Network (GVN), whose goal is to help the international medical community by improving the detection and management of viral diseases.

Bhargavs have recently hit the headlines all over the world with their astounding revelation made through their co-authored book: "Genetically Altered Viruses and Impending Threats to Humanity":

A WORLDWIDE PANDEMIC IS LIKELY TO UNLEASH HAVOC AMONG HUMANS IN ABOUT A DECADE AND ITS SMALLER MANIFESTATIONS MIGHT SURFACE ANY TIME SOON!

The book throws light on a detailed reference to modelling their studies based on stochastic and statistical methods that use the data collected during the previous viral outbreaks in India – the Spanish flu pandemic (Bombay influenza) in 1918-1920, smallpox epidemic in 1974, plague in 1994 and swine flu in 2009. The prediction has sent shock waves through the scientific communities all over the world. However, although the world is going from bad to worse, as far as the infectious viral diseases scenario in the recent past is concerned, governments and policymakers have failed to heed stern warnings like this one!

August – October 2011

The newly elected Prime Minister of India, Dr Sushma Shreshthi, is a leader with a strong vision for her country. She has heard about the book "Genetically Altered Viruses and Impending Threats to Humanity" and is concerned about the prediction. In the meanwhile, the world has witnessed small outbreaks of some unidentified flu as Bhargavs have rightly predicted. As a trained microbiologist, the Prime Minister decided to request Dr Medha and Dr Samyak Bhargav for a meeting in person to get a better insight into their prediction. After the meeting, she is convinced beyond doubt that India will pay dearly if it overlooks this threat. She is one of those leaders who passionately believe in a need to improve one's own country's preparedness in general for outbreaks of emerging and epidemic-prone diseases.

November 2011, New Delhi

An emergency meeting chaired by the Prime Minister of India is underway at an undisclosed location in New Delhi. All union ministers, IEAC members, Prime Minister's Science, Technology, and Innovation Advisory Council (PM-STIAC) are attending the key meeting to debate the possible implications of imminent peril. The marathon meeting being held behind closed doors has culminated in a unanimous consensus among the attendees – a dire need to get into action without any further delay. Various committees assigned with a defined set of action plans are formed along with the creation of a 'Task Force' with immediate effect under the able leadership of the Prime Minister herself.

Dr Medha and Dr Samyak Bhargav have been nominated by The Prime Minister to lead a team of scientists and researchers to work on developing a possible vaccination that can save billions of lives.

December 2011, New Delhi

Prime Minister Dr Sushma Shreshthi addresses the nation, giving its citizens a brief account of the action plan for containing the predicted virus outbreak. She appeals for cooperation and understanding from every citizen. The Prime Minister further urges Indians from all walks of life to contribute generously to the PM CARES fund. She further urges Indian citizens to enter a partnership with the government to solve the challenges of the present and protect the future. Galvanised by the PM's televised address, the nation rises to the occasion. Many industrialists and five of the country's billionaire business magnets pledge to contribute to the PM CARES fund, aimed at strengthening the fight against communicable viral diseases.

January 2012 – December 2018

While some countries in the world are busy fighting against dangerous terrorist organisations, others are engaged in bloody civil wars; a few countries are preoccupied with trade wars with their competitors; many are struggling to cope with the catastrophic consequences precipitated by global warming and climate change; rest are recuperating from the devastating impact of epidemics such as Avian influenza A(H7N9), Ebola, Middle East respiratory syndrome coronavirus (MERS-CoV), Zika virus infection, dengue fever and yellow fever. On the other hand, the Government of India has implemented a series of socio-economic lifestyle change policies in all spheres of day-to-day life, aimed at equipping the nation with a powerful emergency response strategy.

Dr Medha and Dr Samyak Bhargav along with their dedicated team of researchers at IVCR have made significant progress in the development of a Super Combo Vaccination (SCV), capable of boosting the human immunity system defence mechanism so that, it can recognise and combat pathogens – either viruses or bacteria. Researchers are encouraged by two studies in monkeys that offer concrete scientific evidence that surviving Severe Acute Respiratory Syndrome (SARS) may result in immunity from reinfection – a giant leap in the right direction. The team of researchers at IVCR know that they are not too far from achieving their dream!

While the research team at IVCR is working relentlessly in their laboratory, to the world's astonishment, over the last few years, India has managed to transform itself slowly but steadily towards maintaining a delicate balance in nature's biodiversity. It has achieved this balance by embracing green energy sources, eradicating slums in metro cities, controlling the population, decongesting densely populated big cities, reshaping the infrastructure in metro cities, encouraging cottage industries/ agriculture/ farming, conserving forest and wildlife, cleaning up of rivers and water bodies, building an effective basic health care network at the grassroot level, employing technology in mass and distant communications – just to name a few. Under the able leadership of the Prime Minister, social scientists, environmental scientists, scholars in Humanities, technologists, policymakers, government organisations,

NGOs and teams of trained citizen volunteers are engaged in a wide range of activities that have contributed to a 'CLEANER', 'STRONGER' 'HEALTHIER' and 'GREEN' India.

January – October 2019

Dr Medha, Dr Samyak Bhargav and their IVCR team in Bengaluru (Bangalore) have announced the approval of their new, ground-breaking vaccination – SCV, which emerged successfully through all four phases of testing after several initial hiccups. The nation is delighted with the team's feat and joins them in a jubilant celebration! Three of the major Indian pharmaceutical companies were given a patent for the mass production of SCV. It is made available to all primary health care centres across the country - even to the remotest areas. SCV is included as a compulsory vaccination in the National Immunization schedule by the Government of India. Teams of doctors, nurses, paramedics, and trained citizen volunteers gear up for the massive task of inoculating masses with SCV, including newborns.

November 2019

The arduous task of inoculating the masses in the country has been completed. Prime Minister Dr Sushma Shreshthi lauds the collective efforts of the Task Force, scientists, policymakers, technology experts, medical staff, NGOs, volunteers and every individual involved in the action plan. The nation celebrates the well-deserved success that has been realised in a decade-long multi-faceted effort to transform itself and the entire world watches the country in total disbelief!

December 2019

Unfortunately, the time has come to prove Dr Medha and Dr Samyak Bhargav's predictions right! - China announces pneumonia of unknown cause detected in Wuhan, a city in Hubei province and reports it to the WHO Country Office in China on 31 December 2019.

Dr Medha and Dr Samyak Bhargav are perplexed over how to react to the media and the world over the accuracy of their joint prediction - deep in their hearts, they have fervently prayed all through their research work that their calculations would go wrong somewhere, and their predictions would never come true! Ironically, their mathematical model was more precise than they wished it to be!

January 2020: China

China declared the outbreak as a public health emergency of international concern on 30 January 2020. A total of 266 people are infected and the numbers are rising! China imposed a lockdown in Wuhan and other cities of Hubei.

February 2020

On 11 February, WHO announced a name for the new coronavirus disease that appeared in Wuhan as COVID-19 – a cousin of the SARS virus - A novel strain of coronavirus

- SARS-CoV-2. The number of infected people has been rising consistently and the death toll in Wuhan has left the world thunderstruck!

Australia, Japan, South Korea, Singapore, Spain, Italy, France, the UK, and the USA, report positive cases of coronavirus infection and to the world's dismay, the number of deaths due to infection is beyond belief!

The COVID-19 pandemic has unleashed a crisis of global proportions! It has cut across all facets of humanity. It is as if Pandora's box has been forced opened.... evil has engulfed the humans....... utter chaos and despair pervade all over!! May God save this mankind!

India watches the cursed world in horror! It has extended medical support to countries that are desperately in need. COVID's fury continues and seems to be unstoppable.... It has made its way into India...

March-May 2020

The virus has spread at an alarming speed to most of the countries on all the continents by now and the number of infections has risen beyond imagination and shocking death rates have petrified the world!

In India, the number of positive infections continues to be low among citizens. Thanks to SCV, recovery rates are very impressive, and the number of deaths recorded is minimal, as compared to the numbers outside India.

The Indian Prime Minister Smt. Sushma Shreshthi addressed the nation on the 23rd of March. She urges for calm and reassures the nation of its readiness to handle emergency response protocols. The SCV has proved its magic.... It has saved India from what could have been a 'doom's day' otherwise!

PM salutes Dr Medha, Dr, Samyak and the team of scientists and researchers at ICVR for the success of

Super Combo Vaccination. However, considering the highly infectious nature of the virus orders the first phase of the lockdown in the country from 24 March to 14 April. The lockdown later gets extended through April and till the end of May.

Citizens take to working from their homes. Schools, colleges, universities, educational institutes, government offices, and private companies, have adapted to the e-mode using technical know-how and continue to function smoothly. Factories have slowed down on their production owing to the social distance protocols issued by the government. Medical care centres and hospitals are functional with the help of robotic assistants. The giant supply chain of food and essential goods has been efficiently managed by the Task Force with the assistance of armed forces and trained volunteers. Daily wage workers and the poor in the country are provided with temporary shelters, ration supplies and monetary help. While the entire world is railing in fear and uncertainty is brought to a grinding halt, people in India continue to work from home. The country has gotten used to the new norm. Towards the end of May 2020, India slowly started lifting the lockdown, but partially.

The total number of infections in the world continues to grow due to the second wave of infections – the number runs into millions and thousands of people have deceased!! As the world watches the chain of events helplessly, India continues to extend its help to all Asian countries and those countries in need. Experts caution the international communities to follow strict social distancing protocols and urge people to take precautionary measures such as wearing masks and washing hands with soap water to avoid catching infection through contact with various surfaces on which Corvid -19 virus can survive.

June 2020

India has emerged as a clear winner through the pandemic attack saga and is confident of tackling the situation much more efficiently if there is any emergency in the future. All countries are full of appreciation for India and have congratulated the Prime Minister and the citizens for India's decade-long relentless research, planning and far-reaching efforts that have shielded the county against the 'invisible enemy'. India has declared a confident victory over the deadly virus! The world now looks up to India to be its leader in a fight against the lethal grip of the coronavirus.

JULY 2020

The country honours its Task Force team members, scientists, scholars, military personnel, medical staff, NGOs, volunteers and all those individuals who contributed in one or the other way in making the vision come true. Medals of honour have been presented to the front-line fighters.

India has conferred its highest civilian award 'Bharat Ratna' on Dr Medha Bhargav and Dr Samyak Bhargav in an award ceremony held in New Delhi. In their acceptance speech, Bhargavs thanked The Prime Minister for her vision and leadership without which the vaccination alone would not have brought an overwhelming success. Upon being asked to predict possible virus attacks in future and whether they can be eradicated, Dr Medha Samarth replies, "How I wish scientists had a crystal ball to gaze into and forecast what the future holds for humanity! Sadly, despite all the technological advancement to back us up, we do not yet know what is the so-called 'end game' for controlling future pandemics like this one. There is no replacement for research, preparedness, and an effective partnership between leaders, scientists, and citizens. It is this teamwork that plays the most important role in winning impossible wars for the country and hence for humanity. And India has proved this to the world!" We wish that the example that India has set before the world does not go in vain" The audience cheers the country's 'new heroes' with a huge round of applauds that do not seem to fade away any time soon…

ACE+

ACE+

-K. S. Purushothaman

Dr K S Purushothaman (b. 1951) is one of the earliest researchers in Science Fiction Studies in India, starting with an M.Phil. on Ray Bradbury in 1979 and a Ph.D. on Asimov in 1990 both from Madras University. Launched **Indian Assn for Science Fiction Studies** in 1998 and has managed to bring together SF readers, writers and scholars through annual conferences held all over India. He has guided scores of scholars for M.Phil. and PhD. After more than 4 decades of teaching and research, he is settled at Vellore. He continues to promote SF writing, reading and research with a missionary zeal.

I was roaring on the already quietening expressway. The traffic on the road and up the road was thinning as the deadline was nearing. Everyone seemed to be in a hurry to reach their destinations before the curfew.

I was one of those last on my way back home. Of course, I had a valid reason for the delay – the presentation at the UN meeting took longer than expected; I had to answer a lot of questions before the Proposal was passed unanimously. Oh! Sorry. Let me put it in perspective. Well, I am Dr Ramachandran, Head of the UN Committee on Post-COVID-19 Remediation. I am the Director, Dept. of Epidemiology and Virology, Govt. of India. I can say, very proudly, that all the protocols being followed in the "After the Corona Era" remediation were initially designed, implemented and managed by my father and his team. And I can say, modestly, that I am fortunate to continue his good work.

The phone began ringing and I answered, eagerly. As expected, it was Shanti. "Hello, Ram! Where are you? How much longer will it take you to get home? Why should you be the last to get home every time? All the others are here already, and the kids are asking for you, anxiously!" Well, if you let her, she will go on and on! Had to cut through the rushing, gushing chatter. Have always thought of calling her 'My own Venkamma' my dear 'Waterfall Venkamma,' a character in the novel Kanthapura by Raja Rao written in 1938. Somehow the name of this village virago stuck in my mind ever since my father related the story in my schooldays.

Successfully dammed up my wife's talk and managed to tell her that I was on my way and would be home safely and in time. Even as I disconnected the home call, my team's conference call came through. All 20 of them began reporting on their allotted work and their journeys towards home. I could fully intake all the details and pass on new instructions comfortably even as I was hurtling at great speed homewards. The expression, 'at breakneck speed', pinged into my mind, an old and obsolete phrase from the old, pre – Corona days. This too was commonly used by my father from the day he bought me my first bike. Well, now one need not worry about speeding on any road; all vehicles are programmed for protection; and there are no accidents anymore. The traffic on local roads/ expressways is monitored and controlled and of course, all vehicles are self-propelled and auto driven. The passengers just feed in the destinations and relax. They are safely 'delivered'!

Sorry, I digressed. It is always a temptation to extol the new age, referred to as 'ACE': After the Corona Era. It's common knowledge that the Coronavirus pandemic of 2020 drastically changed the world in all its aspects. The demographic composition of the world, especially of India, was transformed, in numbers, social structures and even in psychological perspectives. The agent of all these was the 'Lockdown'! The long periods of containment in different zones and the prohibition of movements had a profound effect on the world. Economic downturns, labour issues, migrant workers and so on. The Lockdown, the right measure to control the spread of viral infection and loss of life, was effective when imposed at an early stage like in India. The govt. was quick and strict in implementing the 'LDs'. Initially, people were upset and careless. Later, the LDs became vibrant centres of change! The cluster concept that became the driving force of LD further added to the positive turn around.

Ah!! Here I am. My car had touched down on the rooftop landing and moved automatically into its shed. I quickly got off with all the gifts and my luggage and stepped into the elevator shaft, drifted or floated gently down to the ground floor living room and walked into my world, my Family. No more the old nuclear families. We had gone back to older times when each family used to be almost a tribe or vice versa. All that had changed with Western culture's infusion into India. Urbanization had further eroded the joint family structure, leading to the Western norm of nuclear families. The outcome was a sad loss of values and sadder gains of materialistic attitudes. A few feeble voices against these debilitating developments were lost in the money market wilderness. But all that changed again for the better, post-Coronavirus and post-LD as people stayed indoors for months, clustered in family groups.

My family, now, clustered around me – older people patting me paternally, the younger ones smothering me in hugs, overwhelming me in a tsunami of love. The epicentre of this cluster was Shanti. Her eyes locked down with mine and instantly I felt a palpable peace descending on me; that is the effect she always had on me! Sure, she had been rightly named!! Next to her were my darling kids, my firstborn gift, now a physician and her younger sibling, a budding AI scholar! Next were my parents, Dad in his 80s and Mom in her late 70s; then Shanti's mom, in her early 70s, who was busy in the kitchen organizing dinner for all. On the outer circle were my siblings: elder brother, wife and two children; my sister and hubby and three kids; Shanti's sister, hubby and two kids. This is the current status of my large family cluster.

There are bigger family clusters these days. I know of one of my friend's families that has about 166 members of 4 generations living together! Sociologists are referring to micro-, macro- and mega-clusters. I am again reminded of a classic Science Fiction, The Caves of Steel, a novel by Isaac Asimov of the 1950s, where mega-enclosed cities accommodated 6 to 8 million people, in a single cluster. I used to wonder what if a coronavirus-like virus got into this steel City. This and other SF novels were my staple diet in my childhood – Dad was an SF fan and I had heard and read voraciously from his library. He was also a scientist and an expert in epidemics and their management. The SF stories inspired him to propose remedial methods to the Indian govt. and to the UN for post-Corona remediation. His concepts were based on the "Ce/Fe" culture that Asimov proposed in The Caves of Steel. Of course, he had recommended a partnership with humans and robots: 'Ce' refs to carbon = human and 'Fe' refs to iron = robot. But Dad saw a different relationship: 'C' = Cluster and 'F' = Family, and together with the 'C/F' Culture. Thus, Clustering became the new term for Family, consisting of many nuclear families.

In one of his first proposals, Dad suggested that LDs can be positively exploited by strengthening and promoting family life as safe, empowering and economically viable. On being approved, this concept was recommended to all nations. The Indian Govt. was quick to pass an ordinance for the new clustering and that such family clusters will be given special status. Gradually, over the years the C/F culture took root, and a new world order began to emerge, where human relationships became a strong binding force.

Today, as I stand immersed in the wave of my family's love, I feel proud that we, Dad and I, are instrumental in effecting this fundamental change. Today is a special day. It is the 50th anniversary of the Lockdown in India – 25th March 2070. Incidentally, it is my birthday too!! I was born on the midnight of 25th March 2020. My pet name, ever since, has been 'Lockdown Ram'!!

It had been proposed that every year on this day the whole country must shut down in a Lockdown of 14 days; everyone should be home with their families before midnight of 25th March every year. Anyone found outside their cluster, without a valid reason, will be quarantined in special camps. Initial hiccups apart, the imposed LDs fostered human relationships as of greater value than material possessions. The negative viral pandemic has been transformed into a positive social change, with all the attendant benefits for the environment. Another proof of human ingenuity that can find solutions to issues in the most unlikely ways.

I heard a whisper, "A penny for your musings, my son. Let the Force be with you". Another softer whisper, "Peace be with you, dear Lockdown Ram. Let us all become one happy 'We' this special LD". That was Shanti. "No! Mr Eliot, the world will not end in a bang or a whimper. It will abide and there will be 'Shantih'!"

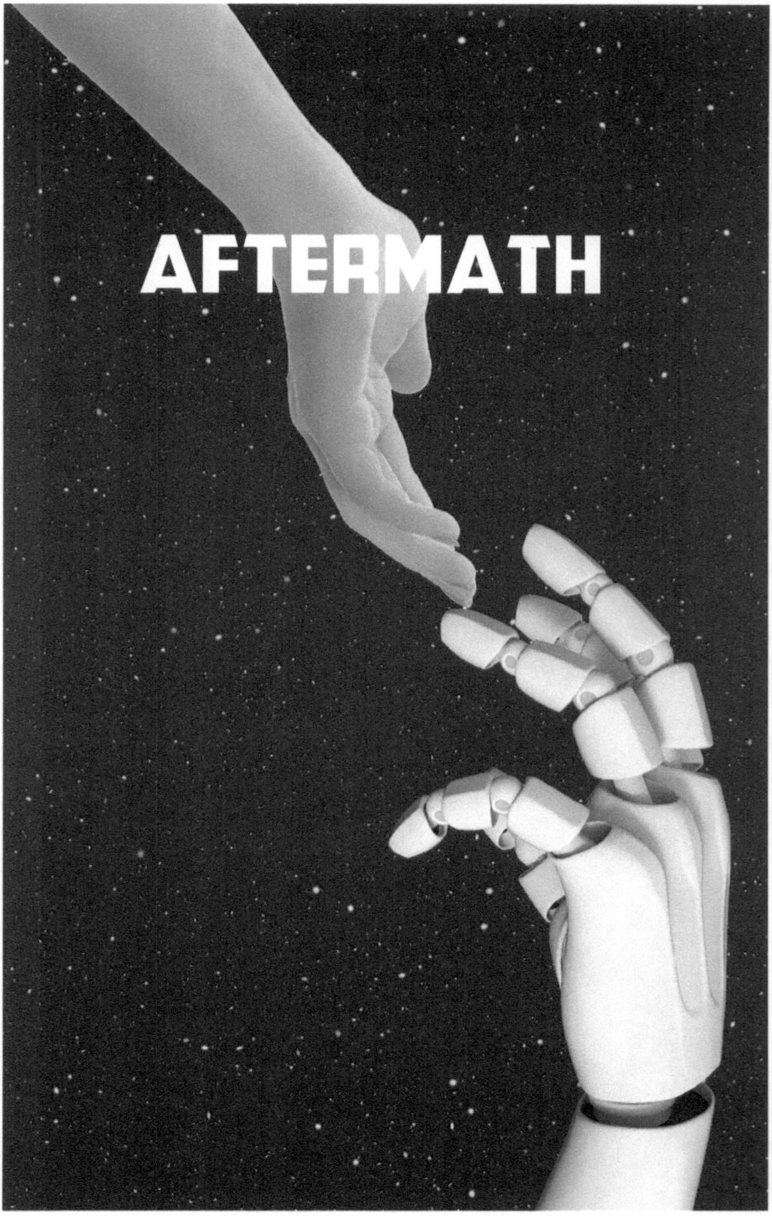
AFTERMATH

AFTERMATH

-Soham Guha

The universe is made of quarks and speculative dreams. As a part of this universe, Soham Guha (সোহম গুহ) finds himself often in his suburban home near Kolkata (India). He writes in his mother tongue, Bengali, and English as well. His works were published in Kalpabiswa, Scroll.in, Mohs 5.5: Megastructure Anthology (Part of Peregrine Lander payload), Mithila Review, Meteotopia: Futures of Climate (In)justice, Rikka Zine, and The Gollancz Book of South Asian Science Fiction Vol II. His collection of Bengali speculative fiction can be found in Archimedes and Other Stories (2022, Kalpabiswa Publications). He is also the editor of speculative fiction and thriller in The Antonym. His upcoming novels, both Bengali and English, are stories he wanted to push through pen for a very long time.

"Hi, I am your Urmila. Pleased to meet you." Prabal looked at the piece of machinery that was delivered to him, a gift from his son who was stuck at the far side of the world. A caregiver robot for the elderly. He sighed; his weathered body didn't permit him to do much work around the house. Cobwebs and litter were found in every nook and corner. It had been eight years since everything that defined humans fell apart. It had been eight years since the COVID pandemic started.

Like every disaster, it too had a humble beginning. Someone somewhere ate something he was not supposed to. In a time of globalization, the disease spread like wildfire that caught Australia only a few months ago of the same year. Now looking back, 2020 was biblical in proportion. Some said it was the beginning of the end of the Kali Yuga.

Prabal looked at the robot and asked, "You are only an upgraded vacuum cleaner. Aren't you?"

Urmila shook her plastic head in response. "No, Prabal. I am here to help you."

#

Prabal knew this day would come. The world was changing faster than he could appreciate. The other day when he went to the bank, after going through the routine hand sanitiser squirts and waiting in a queue while maintaining distance, he was greeted by a robot cashier. However, calling the machine a robot would be an overstatement. Unlike those who were reading the news or the one in his house right now, this kind of machinery did not have a functioning sentience processor. Instead, it was controlled by a person who was able to preserve her job in the economic crisis that followed the pandemic. Like a modified prosthetic, the droid was an extra-anatomical wireless extension of a human who was forced to work from home. In wonder, he asked the cashier, "How's work?"

The cashier replied, "Boring as usual. But 5.5G was timely. Thank god. I can count the money with only a microsecond delay. Please swipe your card and press the amount on the screen with the single-use toothpicks on the counter. Thank you."

Her voice carried a digital rhythm, but Prabal could hear her frustrations from the small opening of the droid's face.

Remembering the cashier, he asked Urmila, "Are you really you? Or there is someone with a controller in her hand who will help me with the household chores?"

Urmila's plastic lips widened. It could easily be mistaken as a smile. "For privacy concerns and security purposes, I am an autonomous unit. Tell me what to do."

The smile was carried to Prabal's face, "There are Toor dal and rice in the cupboard. Just boil them together with salt, if you can."

#

At first, Prabal decided to keep an eye on the kitchen. But after seeing how quickly she – Prabal refrained from calling Urmila 'it' – accustomed herself to Prabal's house, he went to his bedroom and fished out his laptop from the bedside drawer. He opened a video calling application and asked his son when his face appeared, "Hallo, beta. What kind of fresh hell did you send me?"

Mukul saw the worry on his dad's face. It was a long day in Boston, and he was exhausted. He looked at his inviting bed and rubbed his eyes, "It's for your good, papa. Since ma died, you have been a bit – what should I say – cynical."

"I am not losing my mind."

"Papa, here I am with my child and wife. There you are living alone. I couldn't travel to India when the disease got ma. I could not attend her cremation though I very much wanted to. If that feeling can eat me alive, I can only grasp what it is doing to you. We are social creatures.

Unlike my son, we were not moulded since birth for this isolation. We thought there would be a vaccine for Corona within a year, and that we will return to our normal life. In this wait, seven more years have passed, and all our hope has diminished. Thirty lakh people died believing that there will be a cure one day. I ordered this robot to give you company. She is costly, dad, only a second generation of caretakers for elderly people like you. Treat her well, and with care. She is, after all, non-refundable, non-returnable."

"Don't give lectures on diseases, Mukul. I am a doctor."
"A voluntarily retired neurosurgeon, Papa."

Prabal cut the call and sank into his bed. Monsoon reached Kolkata early this year. His busy locality had been quiet for a long time. He counted the sound of falling raindrops on his glass window and soon sleep overcame his anger.

An enchanting smell woke Prabal up. Urmila stood with a tray. He looked at the steaming rice, curry of rohu fish, and the fuming dal and asked, "Who taught you to cook?"

Urmila said, "I have an inbuilt library. I can recite to you everything humans have created in their entirety. If you don't understand the language of the prose, I can translate or summarize it. Some of them are cookbooks. While chopping the scallions, I saw the empty containers of turmeric and black pepper. So, I took the liberty to order a restock online, in the government portal for locally made supplies. The delivery will be here tomorrow."

"You have my Aadhar-linked account number?"

"Since the moment you connected me to your Wi-Fi, I have. I also reconfigured the firewall for added security."

Prabal expected the dishes to be bland. But after he divided the rice into two equal parts, made a small hole in one, poured a portion of the dal and mixed it thoroughly with his hands, and took a mouthful, his taste buds erupted with life. Tears came to his eyes. It tasted just like his wife used to make. The dish was a perfect recreation. He had not eaten anything this good for a long time.

Occasionally he treated himself with foods delivered from restaurants, arriving in sanitized packages; but they were too full of unnecessary spices. They often troubled his old stomach. When there was time, he chose not to learn cooking from his wife. Once he could not imagine a life without her. And now six years without her had gone like a hailstorm.

While eating, how Urmila differentiated himself from humans struck him. After a satisfying burp, he said, "Damn. I forgot to wash my hands before eating."

"It's okay, Prabal. While you were sleeping, I left the food on low heat and cleaned the house. There had been some mites on the sofa but nothing else. Your door lock's log shows you haven't left the house for over a week. You are healthier than most of your age."

It's my mind that is dying, Prabal thought.

#

Slowly, Prabal got adjusted to Urmila. She washed his back, she cooked him food, she recited fiction and articles when he needed to. His television set only ran reruns of old shows and movies. Due to the virus, no cinematography production was possible. Its place was swallowed by a plethora of animated films and anime. Books again became the cultural output of humanity like it was half a century ago. Only the players played in empty stadiums to broadcast the games.

Sometimes Prabal thought of those not so fortunate like him. He had a friend circle but lost steady contact with them when the pandemic hit. It was not wise for people over the sixties to travel across the city for a comforting chat. To add fuel to this misery, almost all of his friends were technologically handicapped. When he told Urmila about this, she said, "I can arrange something."

"How?"

"Prabal," during her time with him, she never called him master. The idea was soothing for Prabal too. "The farmers are growing crops with controlled machinery. The industries are running with fully automated components. You can order anything, and it will arrive at your doorstep by a drone or a self-driven car. You don't need people to sustain your civilization. It took only a microscopic encapsulated, self-replicating strand of RNA to show capitalism is futile. Socialism is the way of the future. If you help each other, and keep your greed in check, the world will live. It will thrive. Because, in the end, the virus isn't choosy about its host. It doesn't prioritize between rich and poor, prophets or hypocrites, moralists or corrupts. It doesn't feel or even care. It just is."

"You were created in Europe. It is easy for you to say things like this. But India is a poor country. If we cannot feed our poor, what is the meaning of living in the future?"

"You don't know about the schemes the government is providing to rural India. The villages are thriving with fiscal stimuli to the MSMEs and agriculture. How do you think the vegetables and cotton dresses reach your doorstep at a reasonable price when shopping malls and MNCs have closed shops? And you're wrong, Prabal. The company responsible for my manufacturing is in France. But I was assembled in Lesotho and all of my parts came from various parts of the world. My shell was made in Vietnam. My silicon hairs were grafted onto my plastic head by workers from Kiribati and Tonga. My processor came from Taiwan. My battery was made in Japan. My other parts were created in South Korea."

"The only parts of the world without disease. A new world order, isn't it?"

"Yes. Your generation wants to dive into the future while keeping a foot in the past. I don't understand why your generation prioritizes physical chitchats over video calls, what makes particular parts of your brain bath in dopamine rain. I cannot make you go to the club where your buddies gathered before. But I can make you close."

Almost all of Prabal's photographs were kept in a physical album. During her time in the house, Urmila scanned and uploaded them in a personal cloud in case of any mishap. Though Prabal was the master of the house, Urmila quickly became the one running it. If she was a human, Prabal couldn't dare to trust her so blindly. Humans will always have external obligations, not robots like her.

It took three days for the package to reach him. When he opened, he found an augmented reality glass and gloves. "A complete suit is also coming," Urmila said when he asked about the delivery. Due to his profession as a doctor, money was not a problem for Prabal. But when he opted to buy the equipment for his friends, almost everyone refused. It was not needed, they said. When they talked, their words sounded like rehearsed dialogues. Time had taken his friends from him. Those who wanted to converse could not. And Prabal understood why. Unlike him, they were in the care of their children. The children did not want their parents to converse with each other again. In a country facing a stern financial crisis, with joblessness rising to almost twenty- two per cent of the available workforce, no children could afford anything unnecessary. Elderlies were always considered liabilities but now the charge of an old age home was not affordable anymore.

In the end, Prabal was left alone in his room, with the gloves, glasses, and suit tucked inside their respective packaging. Urmila asked, "Why don't you use these to connect with your grandchild? They have the necessary toys."

Since his birth, Chandan has been present to Prabal through only video calls and shared photographs. Born in the states, he was an alien to his grandfather. Though he often talked to him via Mukul, there always had been a sea of emptiness to confront Prabal. It was his wife's wish to hold the child before she died. Neither she had the chance, nor it was possible. Prabal saw his wife taking her last breaths cocooned in a plastic isolation sarcophagus. When she died, only her ashes were delivered to Prabal. He could not see her for one last time, even with all the connections he established during his long years of practice. The sea of emptiness only became an abyssal ocean after her death. For the last six years, Prabal was functioning much like Urmila, like a robot made of flesh and bones.

#

"Yes, grandpa, I am wearing the augmented reality suit. Log in and I will be there before you," Chandan said, wearing a smaller version of his suit. Somewhere on the internet, Prabal learned the multifunctional use of the suit.

The prototypes of these suits were first created as 'love-suits' after an online dating platform launched its VVIP mode with an embedded augmentation program. Stranded lovers around the world were able to make love thanks to the suit. Cyber-brothels followed the innovation and soon the world stranded between four concrete walls became almost as close as it was before. Urmila had told him about the latest iteration of the suits, the v6.3.58, manufactured to boost the fallen tourism industry. "With a nasal attachment included with the other instruments, the suit will take you anywhere in the world. You can walk on the top of Mount Everest or run from the lions at Serengeti. Of course, none of it will be real but the barrier between real and virtual will be even blurrier," she had added.

"Hi, grandpa," a soft, humble voice spoke as soon as Prabal wore the earphones. After he put his glass on, Chandan appeared in his drawing-room. He was taller than his age, due to the printed food becoming mainstream in the states. When Prabal walked to him and patted on his head, it felt real. He felt his soft hair, the warmth of his skull. Tears came to his eyes and Prabal said, "You have your grandma's eyes."

For more than four hours, Prabal talked with Chandan. Chandan told him about his online augmented reality classes and how many friends he made. There was, as always, a bully and a girl he liked.

"Who's she?" Prabal asked and he immediately spotted the reddening of Chandan's cheeks. They have sleepovers, joint study sessions, and even gully cricket with other children of Indian origin – just like he used to have in his childhood days. Though the events were performed with the help of gadgets, Prabal now knew they were as real as they could be.

He asked Chandan, "Have you read any Bengali novels?"

Chandan tapped on a screen popping up near him and showed him his virtual library.

Prabal was pleased to notice many of his favourite novels on the shelves and even more pleased to see the 'already read' tag on some of them. "My mother bought me these. She often picks up a book and tells me the story before I go to bed."

"Stories – art in a broader sense – define our humanity, Chandan. The creative spark makes us different from the machines we created and the animals that came before us. Your father works in the graphite industry, he will have a better knowledge of how these technologies change us without changing who we are. Ask him. But before that, tell me, have you read Chander Pahar (Mountain of the Moon)?"

When Chandan shook his head, Prabal asked Urmila to narrate the story to the boy. Urmila connected a cable with Prabal's suit and started to tell Chandan the enthralling story of Shankar and his quests through the uncharted parts of Africa in search of diamonds with an old Portuguese prospector named Alvarez. Her storytelling took Prabal almost thirty years back: his wife was telling young Mukul the same story and he was watching them from behind a curtain.

Like his father, Chandan's eyes also widened when the narrative took Shankar to encounter the ferocious beast Bunyip.

When Urmila finished the long novel, Prabal hugged his grandchild tightly and said, "Goodbye for now. Tomorrow there will be another story. I promise."

Chandan asked, "Father said you were a doctor. Why did you stop being one?"

His heart ached while answering and her wife's smiling face appeared in his mind. "Because, Chandan, even with all my knowledge, I was not enough to save your grandmother."

After disconnecting the suit, he found himself with sore eyes and an aching back. The evening had given way to a late night.

"I will make something quick, for dinner," Urmila said.

"Don't bother, I am not hungry," Prabal said with a sour tongue.

Urmila stopped, her non-moving eyes looking at him, "Pardon me for asking for it is not my place. But as your caregiver and psychological support, it is my obligation. Why did you retire from your work? The virus took most of your doctors, nurses, bank employees, essential workers, and police. Even after eight years, there is a severe deficit in the number of doctors in the country. Why did you feel the need to do so?"

"You are not blessed with a human heart, neither its joy nor its pain. You will not understand." Prabal slowly said. "Now, can you please leave me alone for the night? I am tired."

#

A few days later, Urmila fetched an article for Prabal. She said, "Hawking declared that after 2100, the human population will see a massive decline. Looks like the virus shifted the timeline."

Prabal went through the article quickly. The steady declining birth rates and slowly rising mortality rates caught his eye. "It was bound to happen," he said. "None wants to bring their children into this world where our freedom has become fiction. The other day you asked why I didn't subscribe to the virtual tourism program. Even with the suit, the augmentation only will give me a finite soothing. The thrill of booking the tickets, waiting for the train to arrive and then riding it, staying at a place far from home and finding joy in all these, is now absent. It felt like losing a limb as I once was an extensive traveller."

The familiar ringtone of his unused mobile appeared like a raging bull in the silent room. Urmila received the call. "Yes. I will ask him. Certainly." She looked at Prabal while holding the phone in her palm.

"What?" he asked.

"A boy of age fourteen was admitted to Burdwan Medical College. They need your expertise."

"Tell them to fuck off. This is the twentieth time someone called me to perform surgery. I will not entertain another patient in my lifetime." Prabal's voice quickly became rusty.

"You don't understand, Prabal. This kid has a tumour in his hippocampus. They already mailed you the bloodwork and MRI."

"Why, Urmila? Why are you doing this to me?"

"Do you know why I am called Urmila?"

"Named after Lakshman's wife, to give a sense of familiarity. Why else?

"No, Prabal. She was abandoned by her husband for ten years, in the prime of her youth. She was a neglected character in Ramayana. They named me so to make me an integral part of certain Indian households. So, I can justify my presence. Listen to me. I don't understand why you stopped practising; nor do I care. But I know this: there is a boy worth saving. You cannot change the world, but you must try to sustain it."

"You don't understand," Prabal said while looking at the MRI. "The tumour is pressing hard on the brain. There is internal bleeding. The trains are not functioning. Or did you forget that too? Even if I want to go out, it will take me more than three hours to reach. By then, it will be too late."

"There is another way." "What?"

"Put on your suit and equipment. I am now asking the hospital to arrange the output relays."

"Stop, Urmila. This is absurd. Brain surgery is delicate. I cannot risk another's life for some technological malfunction. There will be a delay in the data transfer. My hands might damage another part of his brain within that time."

In response, Urmila unscrewed her chest plate and attached the cables of Prabal's suit with her circuit core. "But you certainly can risk his life by not attending.

Listen, I found one of my models in the hospital. She will be your extension. I heard faith is a human instrument. I believe in you, Prabal. Now you have to believe me."

Prabal wore his glasses and Urmila whispered in his ears. "I reconfigured the internet access. With AI optimization, you are in control of the whole bandwidth. There will be no response delay."

Like a person struck by lightning, he felt minuscule jolts in his suit. He found himself in an operation theatre. The head-nurse said with a smile, "Glad to have you here, doctor."

He looked at his newfound plastic hands and noticed the absence of the trembles his old age gifted him. Urmila was doing her best to exclude any errors from their side. Prabal said, "Thank you for calling me." Unknown to him, his mind was, at last, waking up from a deep slumber.

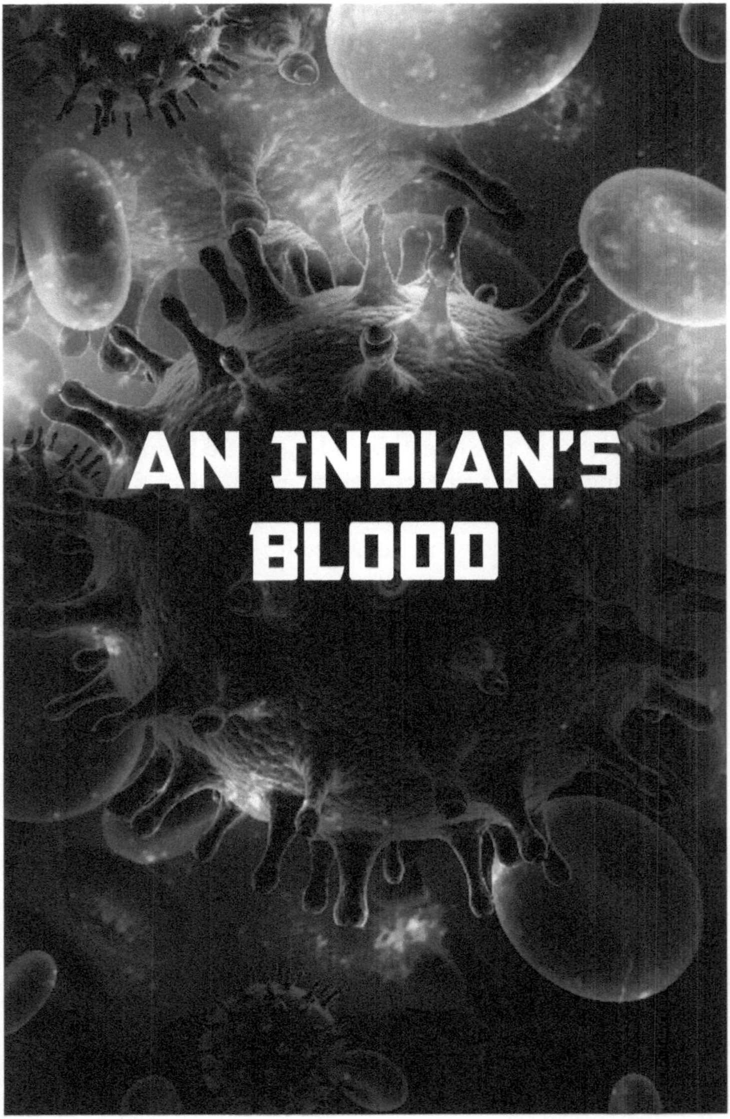
AN INDIAN'S
BLOOD

AN INDIAN'S BLOOD

-Subha Das Mollick

Subha Das Mollick is a filmmaker, writer and professor of Film Studies and Media Studies. Having retired from her full-time engagement as Head of the Media Science Department at iLead Institute, she is presently attached to Aliah University and Viswa Bharati University as a visiting faculty. She did her post-graduation in Physics from Delhi University and was a Physics teacher for 12 years before switching her career to teaching and practising media.

March 16, 2020, Kolkata

The time on the wall clock ticking in the dark bedroom showed 6 O'clock – time for five-year-old Ritika to get out of bed and get ready for school. Ritika's mother Subhadra tiptoed into the room; but instead of waking Ritika up, she tucked the blanket nicely over Ritika and said, "You can sleep a little longer.

Your school is closed today." Ritika replied in her sleep-soaked voice, "Thank you, Mummy. But why?" "An order has been passed", said Subhadra, "Nobody will get out of the house".

"What fun!" Ritika mumbled and went back to sleep.

Later that day, as her mother was busy with kitchen chores and her father sat in front of the TV with a serious face, Ritika laid out her zoo in her playroom. Elephant, huggy bear, gruffy doggie, Bandu monkey, fluffy squirrel – all were out. Even the dolphin was out. Ritika floated it in her little plastic swimming pool. Ritika spent the whole day in the zoo with only a short lunch break. There was nobody to break her spell. Mother was too busy in the kitchen; the maid did not come to clean the room. Ritika only missed her Nani. Ritika loved to hear Nani's rhymes on monkey and dolphin, on bear and squirrel.

Soon the clock struck 5 and it was time to go for a swim. Ritika quickly got up and took out her swimming trunk from the wardrobe. She told Bandu monkey, "Today is your turn. I will take you to the pool." Just then mother rushed into the room and said, "Oh! No, Ritika. We are not allowed to step out of the house. Don't you get it?

No swimming, no karate, no dance class. Everything is closed."

Mummy rudely threw the swimming trunk back into the wardrobe. Ritika was on the verge of tears. "Ritika, there is a monster lurking outside. Its name is Corona. C for Corona. The Corona is so small that we cannot see it. Maybe there are hundreds of thousands of them floating in the air. If you go out, they may settle on your hair, on your dress. They may even get into your body when you breathe in", mother continued excitedly.

Ritika forgot to cry and listened to her mother with her mouth wide open. So, small that one cannot see? Hundreds of thousands of them? Ritika could not make head or tail of what her mother was saying.

Mother continued, "And if they enter your body, they will make you sick. Coughing, high fever and much more. You don't want these tiny monsters to swarm in our home. Do you?"

Ritika hugged her bear in fear. Mother said, "Come. I will take out that expensive tea set from the loft.

Let me quickly finish my work, and then we will play together."

In the living room, daddy was glued to the TV. Ritika could overhear the word 'corona'. She peeped out and saw a green ball-like thing on the TV screen. The ball had strange things sticking out of it. Ritika wondered, "The tiny monsters cannot be seen, mother said. So, who has drawn these monsters and who has painted them green?"

That night, as her mother put Ritika to bed, Ritika wanted to hear a bedtime story – Corona's story. Mother settled down beside her and began her story ….

Far far away, in a land called China, there is a city called Wuhan. The Yangtze River flows past Wuhan. It is an ancient city, but also a very new city with skyscrapers, factories, swanky streets and lots and lots of people. There is a big lake in the east of the city, with tall trees all around the lake. One day…

Ritika was all ears. Subhadra continued:

One day, after it was dark, a bat flapped its wings and settled on the branch of a tree. It was a horseshoe bat. Its face was like the hoof of a horse. But the bat was not feeling too well. It had a slight fever.

"What is a bat?" Ritika asked.

"Not your cricket bat", mother said, "This bat is hairy, and it has wings. Bats can see at night, and they sleep all through the day, hanging from branches of trees."

"So, why was this horseshoe bat unwell?" Ritika asked.

"Because the tiny Corona monsters had entered its body and started doing mischievous things."

Now Ritika got really scared. She covered her head with the blanket and hugged her mother.

Mother's voice trailed off…. The horseshoe bat had fought with a pangolin before settling on this treetop.

"P A N D O L I N?" asked Ritika

"No. P – A – N – G – O – L – I - N. It looks like a big scaly lizard. But it is not a lizard", explained Subhadra.

"The feverish bat fought with the pangolin in the dead of night. Its warm breath fell on the pangolin's face. After injuring the pangolin, the bat flew off and settled on the top branch of the tree.

Down below, the injured pangolin lay curled up in the bush. At daybreak, a man tiptoed from behind and grabbed the scaly mammal…

Ritika's breathing became more even. She had dozed off. Subhadra switched off the night lamp and left the room.

March 16, 2020, New York

Halfway across the world, it was time for Pratiksha to get out of bed and get ready for the hospital. For the last three years, she has been an attending psychiatrist at Bellevue Hospital, NYU School of Medicine.

Right now, the medical community in New York is in a state of emergency. Tests for COVID had begun in right earnest. Hospitals were gearing up to admit patients – isolating the COVID wards from the rest of the hospital, increasing the number of ICU beds and so forth.

Pratiksha had a quick breakfast and braced herself for one more day of challenge. Her grandfather's portrait hung from the wall above. Pratiksha's grandfather used to be a doctor in the Indian Army. He received the Param Vir Seva Medal in 1976. Pratiksha took one look at her grandpa before she left the apartment – as if to seek his blessing for the difficult days ahead.

The public facilities in America had started closing down one by one. All conferences had been cancelled; public gatherings had been banned. Pratiksha walked all the way to her hospital – all 20 blocks of the way. From a distance, she could see the ambulance entering her hospital. One more COVID patient? "Andrew's pressure is building up", Pratiksha said to herself.

One hour into her duty, Pratiksha was counselling one of her old patients. Fear of the COVID pandemic had taken a grip on this 65-year-old lady, who lived all alone. All kinds of messages and videos were crisscrossing in social media. This lady had got a WhatsApp message about the symptoms of the COVID-19 attack. Pratiksha tried explaining to her, "Mrs Stevenson, the first thing you will have to do is, increase your body's immunity system. Eat healthy food, do light exercises, sleep well and stop worrying. If you worry, you will become more vulnerable to the Corona attack. If you stay cheerful, the virus will not be able to have a grip on you." Mrs Stevenson at the other end of the line did not seem convinced. Pratiksha continued, "Yes, Mrs Stevenson. The first signs are a dry cough and a slight itch in the throat. …. What? Do you want to get yourself tested? OK. Please come over to The Bellevue tomorrow.

I am booking the 10:30 time slot in your name."

As Pratiksha hung up, Andrew entered her chamber and said that a new patient had been admitted. He was 60 years old, with a travel history. Perhaps Pratiksha's encouraging pep talk would cheer him up. Andrew was in charge of the COVID-19 ICU. Pratiksha was happy to be of help to Andrew. She quickly put on her PPE, wore her N95 mask, put on her goggles and headed for the ICU with Andrew.

In the ICU, a total of three beds were occupied. Fortunately, nobody had to be put on a ventilator yet. This new patient's heart rate was irregular, he could barely speak. His body temperature was 102 degrees Fahrenheit. Glenn Mills, as written on the patient card, was visibly in great discomfort.

Pratiksha and Andrew felt helpless. They could not touch him or hold his hand. But Pratiksha quickly put on her gloves and took his hand in hers. She knew from her experience that handholding always had a therapeutic effect. "Glenn, you are a fighter. You will fight back. We are there with you", she tried to sound optimistic.

At another bed in the other corner of the ICU, one patient was coughing uncontrollably through his mask. The attending nurse rolled up his bed to make him upright. She gave him some hot water to sip.

Walking along the long corridor leading from the ICU to Pratiksha's room, Andrew informed her that Glenn Mills had a history of a heart ailment. He had had a mild heart attack two years back. So, Sorbitrate had been given to him to stabilize his heart condition. Fortunately, his 58-year-old wife has tested negative. But she has been quarantined – and strictly prohibited from visiting the hospital.

'It is this isolation that is killing", said Pratiksha. "It is terrible not to be able to see your near and dear when you feel so down and low."

Andrew and Pratiksha walked side by side in their 'space suits', both deeply immersed in their thoughts. Seven years of medical training and two years of internship had not prepared them for a situation like this.

At the end of the corridor was Flavia's room. She managed the medicine store. Andrew and Pratiksha stopped by. "Flavia, I hope you are well stocked with paracetamols and multivitamins. Every patient has to be given his daily dose of a multivitamin. That will help to strengthen their immune system."

Flavia showed the stock to Andrew and informed him, "A fresh consignment of HCQ drugs has also been added to our stock." Andrew shrugged his shoulders and pointed to Pratiksha, "That stock is straight from her country. She would know better".

Pratiksha ignored Andrew's snide remark and changed the topic. "How is your daughter, Flavia?" she asked. "Her school is closed, I guess. How is she spending her time at home?"

Flavia pulled the drawer and showed some sketches made by her daughter – funny faces, cheerful

faces, faces that refused to come under the strains of the times. "I must show these sketches to Mrs Stevenson", remarked Pratiksha. "These will surely elevate her spirits."

"Two days back when I went home, I found that she had painted a big rainbow on the windowpane", Flavia said in reply.

That evening, as she walked back home with tired steps, Pratiksha knew that it would be a long-drawn battle for all of them. They were all entering a dark tunnel. Would they emerge out of it unvanquished? God alone knew.

Back home, Pratiksha turned on the TV. The newscaster announced that so far in the USA, there were 50 deaths reported due to COVID-19, as opposed to 3,619 pneumonia deaths. Clearly, the White House was downplaying the situation. Trump's statement of the day was, "It's a very contagious virus, but we have tremendous control over it."

Indeed!! Pratiksha said to herself. The newscaster went on to give details about the race to develop a vaccine. At the New York School of Medicine too, the research was on developing the vaccine.

Pratiksha switched off the light and thought of the rainbow that Flavia's daughter had drawn on her windowpane. 'Hope is what keeps us all alive', was her last thought before sinking into sleep.

April 15, 2020, Kolkata

Subhadra rummaged through Ritika's wardrobe and pulled out a new dress gifted by her auntie on her birthday. Today was Nabo Barsho – Bengali New Year and everybody was supposed to wear a new dress. Thank God this new dress was there for Ritika.

Subhadra kept the bright blue frock on the bed and her gaze fell on Ritika's zoo. There were two new additions – a bat and a pangolin. The pangolin was cut out from one of the animal books. Ritika had told her father to cut it out neatly and paste it on cardboard. Her dad had fixed a stand at the back. So, now the pangolin could stand like a picture frame. The bat had been made with dad's old eye patch.

The eye covers served as the wings of the bat and the body was made with plasticine.

"If the lockdown had not happened, these innovations would never have surfaced", Subhadra thought. She called out to Ritika, "Ritika, quickly have a bath and put on your new dress. Today is Nobo Borsho. We'll deck up our home nicely."

"Nobo Borsho!! So, Nana Nani will come. Yay!!!!"

"Beta, how can they come? We are all locked down, beta. Not allowed to move out of our homes."

Ritika pulled a long face. She hadn't met Nani for ages. Subhadra too suppressed a sigh. But to cheer herself up, she took out the dry colours, the chalk powder and went to her doorstep to make a nice, colourful rangoli. Ritika followed her mother close at heels.

As Subhadra's fingers played with the colours, her thoughts hovered between the past and future. Much had happened in the last month. Online classes had started in the schools. In addition to all the household chores, Subhadra had to take four hours of class on Zoom every day. And for taking these classes, she had to prepare PPTs and other study material till late at night. Subhadra was at wit's end when she had to welcome the new Class XI batch on Zoom. Normally she initiated this class through role play. But over Zoom this was not possible. So, she had to invent new ways to grab their attention.

Ritika too had a one-hour class every day. One day it was EVS, the next day language, the third-day arithmetic and the fourth-day music. Ritika had to put on her school dress before taking her seat in front of her mother's phone. Her friends were there in tiny squares inside the phone. Sometimes she waved at them.

Subhadra's thoughts were interrupted by the phone. Her mother was calling to wish Shubho Nobo Borsho. "Ritika, Nani on video call", she called out to her daughter. "Wish her Happy New Year".

Nani showed all the goodies she had prepared for the occasion – a jar of coconut laddus that Ritika could savour after normalcy returned, a box full of nimkis and the special pancakes with almonds and raisins. Ritika, in turn, held up her colourful fingers to Nani.

Fifteen kilometres away, at a one-storeyed bungalow in Salt Lake, an old-fashioned telephone rang.

Eighty years old Jaya had been sitting patiently by the phone, expecting this call. She picked up eagerly and said, "Shubho Nobo Borsho, Pratiksha dear, my pretty child. How are you?"

But what is this? From the other side, instead of the usual cheerful voice, Jaya head a sob. Pratiksha could barely speak. In between her sobs, Pratiksha said, "Nani, Flavia is no more."

"Who?" Jaya asked.

"Our medicine store manager. Flavia. She is the latest COVID-19 victim in our hospital. I can't figure out

how Flavia, of all people, caught the infection. And she has left behind a teenaged daughter."

Even though Pratiksha spoke from thousands of miles away, her granddaughter's fear and anxiety were all too palpable to Jaya. All she did was utter a prayer, a hymn to

Lord Krishna, that she had taught to Pratiksha as a child. The hymn, if uttered in good faith, always gave strength to face adverse situations.

Jaya said, "Take care, my child. Your grandfather's blessings will always be with you" and hung up.

She sat by the phone like a statue. Pratiksha was all alone in New York. Come what may, she would have to brave it all by herself. But she was a brave child, much like Jaya's late husband, Brigadier R.N Dutta. Grandpa used to tell Pratiksha, "When you grow up, you will be a doctor. You will serve humanity with all your soul."

In Subhadra's house, the tiny family of three settled down for their Nobo Borsho lunch. They vowed to stay cheerful and talk about happy things. Subhadra's husband recalled a funny incident that had happened on last year's Nobo Borsho day. Ritika went into peals of laughter.

April 17, 2020, New York

"Happy Birthday, pretty", Andrew said in a cheerful voice as he walked into Pratiksha's room with a bunch of freshly plucked flowers. He put the flowers in a vase and greeted Pratiksha with an Indian namaste.

"What's the situation upstairs?" asked Pratiksha in reply. "It's house full. Every single bed occupied", replied Andrew "And ventilators?"

"Three of them are on ventilators".

"Come, let's go for a round. They should keep their hope alive until..." "The end?"

Pratiksha lowered her head.

"How many have recovered under your care?" She asked Andrew.

"More than 60%, by a rough estimate," Andrew said with some pride. "Glenn Mills went home one week back. He fought a long-drawn battle, but he won."

"That's good", Pratiksha said, as she put on her PPE and mask. "Despite having a history of weak heart, he fought it out."

The two of them walked past Flavia's room with a heavy heart. How she succumbed to COVID-19 had remained a mystery to all the staff. One day she felt dizzy and fell flat on her face as she tried to get up from her seat. She tested positive. She was admitted to the COVID ward and within ten days she was gone.

Inside the ICU, a nurse was turning over a patient on a ventilator. Pratiksha rushed to help the nurse. This turning over had to be done at regular intervals, to make sure that both lungs got ventilated. This patient was a big man. And he was barely conscious.

"After Flavia's death, the hospital staff has got badly demoralized", Andrew later told Pratiksha. "Maybe a counselling session has to be arranged for them. On Zoom or something."

"But they are so busy! Do you think they will have time for a counselling session? But hold on…."

Pratiksha had an idea. "We can tell the hospital management to make 'thank you' cards for each one of them. Each card can have a unique message."

"Brilliant!!!" Andrew said admiringly. "Tomorrow when they report to work, each one of them will get an envelope – a thank you card with a special message."

That evening, Andrew and Pratiksha stayed back at the hospital long after their duty hours were over. They spent a lot of time in the ICU and spoke to the nurses individually.

At the far end of the day, they settled down with a cup of coffee and brought up the topic of vaccines.

"I am not hopeful about the development of a vaccine", Andrew opined. "Even after 39 years, we do not have a vaccine for AIDS"

"And even after 70 years, we do not have a vaccine for Zika virus. The chickenpox vaccine was developed 42 years after the virus appeared on the face of the earth. The Hepatitis vaccine was discovered after 16 years, and the Ebola vaccine was successfully tested only last year. There is no vaccine yet for the SARS virus", Pratiksha gave out the long list.

"Yes. The SARS virus appeared in 2003. It was a less virulent predecessor of COVID-19." "There is a 99% similarity between the SARS CoV and SARS CoV 2. With just 1% alteration in its

genome structure, it has turned so virulent. This time it jumped from bats to pangolins to humans!!

There is 96% to 98% similarity between the virus found in bats and the ones that are infecting us." "Frankly, I am not so sure of the origin of COVID."

'Don't tell me, you believe in the conspiracy theory going around – Trump's China virus theory!"

"I don't know, Pretty! I don't know. All I know is that we are under the grips of the most contagious virus the world has ever known and we do not have a defence against it. We have to fight on without any shield, any sabre, any weapon."

Andrew gave a deep sigh. The two of them took the last sip of their coffee, threw the paper cups in the incinerator bin and got up to go.

May 1, 2020, Kolkata

It was midnight. Subhadra was making preparations for the next day's class. Ritika too was wide awake. She was giving company to her mother. Ritika picked up the green crayon and drew a coronavirus in her drawing book. She had drawn it so many times that by now she was an expert in drawing the virus.

In the evening Daddy had explained to her how the virus enters the human body through the nostrils and attacks the lungs. Ritika took out that page where Daddy had made the drawing and started explaining to her mother, "Look, this is how the corona creeps into our lungs."

"What are lungs, beta?"

"Balloons inside our chest"

"Very good. And how do you keep the corona from entering our lungs?" "By wearing masks".

"Very good. Tomorrow, you have your personal hygiene class. Please show these drawings to your teacher and also show her your mask."

May 5, 2020, New York

Back home in her apartment after yet another back-breaking day, Pratiksha took off her mask and settled down with the latest issue of Lancet. Today, another patient succumbed to COVID-19 in her hospital. What is worse, a couple of hospital attendants had been infected. With less hospital staff for service, those who were still healthy had to be on duty for 12 hours a day – on their toes for all 12 hours, running from bed to bed – and the end of the ordeal was not in sight. Today Andrew was also looking tired. There were dark circles around his eyes.

She flipped the pages of the Lancet to know more about the nature of the virus playing havoc with the human respiratory system. What is problematic about the COVID-19 virus is that it modifies its outer protein cover very fast, making it nearly impossible to develop a vaccine. Already there were eighty thousand COVID deaths in the USA and nearly three hundred thousand deaths all over the world.

Pratiksha's grandfather, Brigadier R.N Dutta had been a haematologist. He had earned fame for developing an antidote for snake venom. Pratiksha remembered her grandfather saying that the antidote had been developed from the antibodies in the plasma of horses. Only horses could survive snake bites

Pratiksha took out her little diary and made a note. "Tomorrow morning I'll have a chat with the pathologist", she resolved before switching off the light.

The next morning as she switched on her phone, Andrew's message was awaiting her: 'I am quite sick. Dizziness, diarrhoea and all. Will get myself tested today.'

Pratiksha had seen this coming. She saw the message and made up her mind. She would now volunteer for full-time emergency service.

Pratiksha walked briskly to the hospital and waited for Andrew to arrive. On the way to the testing lab, Andrew asked Pratiksha, "Why don't you get yourself tested too?"

"What's the use? Positive or negative, I'll have to do my duty. Besides, I live alone, more or less a quarantined life. There is no fear of infecting anybody."

At night Pratiksha called up her granny and informed her that Andrew had tested positive, he was quarantined, and she was stepping into Andrew's shoes. Pratiksha would now be the superintendent of the COVID ward. She had volunteered for this position.

Jaya felt proud and anxious. She went to the Puja room for her morning prayers and began reciting the Krishna hymn.

May 15, 2020, Kolkata

Deep into the night, Subhadra could hear the wailing of the ambulance. She went to the balcony to check out. The ambulance entered their building premise and two men wearing PPE got down. After some time, they wheeled out Mr Bhattacharya from Wing A. Nemai Bhattacharya used to be a renowned writer. Now he was in a wheelchair. He lived alone with his caretaker. Two days back when

Subhadra went to the market to buy daily provisions; she had met the caretaker. But he did not mention anything about Mr Bhattacharya's illness!

Subhadra came back to her room. She could feel the palpitation in her chest. Her throat felt dry. Would she wake up her husband and tell him? No. Let him sleep in peace.

Subhadra sat in the darkroom for a very long time. All kinds of thoughts rushed through her mind. In the wee hours of the morning, her nerves felt a little calm. She went to the bedroom and lay down.

The next morning it was there in the papers. Regent Park had been declared a containment zone. Their building had been cordoned off. Nobody was allowed to go in or out.

Subhadra went down to get the milk packet delivered at the entrance of the building. When she came up, Ritika was awake. She saw her mother and said, "Mummy, did you go down to get the laddus that Nani has made for me?"

Subhadra was too tired and anxious to smile. She said, "Beta, the laddus will stay for one more month, I am sure". Under her breath, she muttered, "Just pray that things come back to normal by then".

May 31, 2020, New York

Patrick Young had been wheeled in a while ago. A big black man, he was definitely this side of 60. But he was in bad shape. His neighbour had accidentally discovered him, lying in a nearly unconscious state on the front porch of his home.

Patrick was put on a ventilator immediately. His blood pressure was fluctuating, his pulse was irregular. His medical history was as yet not known. Pratiksha spent some time by this man's bedside and kept an eye on the ECG monitor. His chest was heaving up and down like a bellow.

In the next bed, there was a 67-year-old professor. He had been admitted two days back, but his condition was deteriorating. When he had been brought in, he had cheerfully quoted a line from Shakespeare. Pratiksha and Professor played a game of optimistic characters and pessimistic characters in Shakespeare's plays. Now Professor was lying almost lifeless.

Pratiksha looked around. Every single bed was occupied. Every patient was heaving for breath. It was past midnight, but there was no question of going home now. Suddenly her eyes fell on bed number 3. One of the hospital workers was occupying this bed. He had tested positive a week back and two days back he had to be admitted to the ICU. A chill ran down Pratiksha's spine.

June 15, 2020, Kolkata

Kolkata was now three months into locked down state, although the lockdown had been eased in pockets. In many places, people simply disregarded the norms. They crowded in marketplaces and gathered at wayside tea stalls.

Subhadra was extremely busy making preparations for the remaining board exams. The exams would start in a fortnight. For the first time board exams would be held online. The exams, abruptly truncated three months back, would now be completed. The students were relieved, but also anxious about the new format.

Ritika's school had not yet started, but her online classes had resumed after summer vacations. Three months of a five-year-old's life spent completely indoors. She now became a movie guzzler – watching at least two movies in a day.

Subhadra sometimes wondered – was this prolonged lockdown necessary? In a country like India, we have developed a tough immunity system. We cohabit with so many diseases. She looked at

Ritika wondered what the future of these children would be. Would their childhood be snatched from them forever?

June 30, 2020, New York

The death toll in the USA had crossed a hundred thousand. In Bellevue itself, more than 100 COVID-19 deaths have occurred in the last four months. For Pratiksha and all the other caregivers at the hospital, it was 14 hours of duty on all seven days of the week. Andrew had recovered, but he was very weak. He had been advised one more week's rest. Pratiksha had to hold the fort till then.

It was lunchtime and lunch was being served to all the patients. Very few of them were in a position to sit up and eat. The nurses made an effort to feed them with a spoon. Pratiksha too quickly finished her lunch. But as she got up, suddenly her head spun, and she fell down. Everything blacked out.

Ten years later

Ritika was now a young lady of 15, getting ready for her board exams. Like her mother, she too wanted to be a schoolteacher. But school was very different from what it used to be in her mother's time. Her mother often told stories of students rolling on the grass at lunchtime, sitting together in groups and sharing each other's lunch, she spoke of the packed hall on the first day of school, the overflowing school bus taking the children home. Now the students go to school every other day. They stayed in school for barely four hours. Masks had become a part of the school dress. The schoolbook had elaborate instructions to follow social distancing. It was explained with diagrams how students should sit far apart in the classroom, and how they should maintain distance in the playground. There was no such thing as an assembly. Prayers happened in respective classrooms. The principal could be seen and heard on CC TV in every classroom. During the sports period, they ran along the tracks maintaining a one-metre distance from each other, they did gymnastics on mats spread out at distances of 6 feet.

And on the days, they stayed at home, they watched the pre-recorded lectures on the school portal.

Subhadra often wondered if schooling with social distancing would really serve the purpose of schooling. Socializing was an important aspect of schooling. Bonding between friends, and peer learning was a part of growing up. What memories of growing up would these children bear? They were only learning to interact with artificial intelligence and virtual avatars of their friends. Of course, Subhadra had to come to school every day and stay on for long hours recording videos, uploading them and so much more.

Today she went home and switched on the TV by force of habit. But the newscaster's announcement caught her attention:

THE VACCINE FOR COVID 19 IS AT LAST HERE. AN INDIAN DOCTOR, DR PRATIKSHA MITRA, PLAYED A KEY ROLE IN THE DEVELOPMENT OF THIS VACCINE.

"Ritika, come here, there is big news", Subhadra shouted.

Mother and daughter sat down to watch the news. Dr Pratiksha Mitra was there in the studio. An American pathologist joined from his lab in the USA. Dr Mitra spoke about the difficult months she had spent in 2020 at the Bellevue Hospital in New York. All the medical staff attending to the patients were getting sick one by one. Pratiksha was the last one to fall.

The pathologist from the USA said that Pratiksha had given official notification to the pathology lab that if she contracted Corona and recovered from the disease, pathologists should collect her blood and extract the plasma. Perhaps they would get the antibodies they were looking for.

Pratiksha, sitting in the TV studio, gave a vivid description of her 15-day-long battle with the disease. She had triumphed in the end. At the end of the long, dark tunnel, she could see light. During those 15 days, her friend Andrew kept her morale up and her grandmother from India called every day and said that she was proud to have Pratiksha as her granddaughter. One day she sent a recording of the story that Pratiksha was so fond of hearing as a child. Pratiksha was sure that her Indian genes and the constant moral support had pulled her out of the abyss.

The American pathologist explained what they had done with Pratiksha's blood sample – how they had preserved the plasma using cryogenic techniques. Now the vaccine was ready for public use. This would be America's gift to the world. Just like the polio vaccine, this would become mandatory for children all across the globe.

The newscaster made his concluding remarks:

THE MUCH-AWAITED VACCINE IS AT LAST HERE. IT WILL HOPEFULLY BRING BACK NORMALCY IN MANY SPHERES OF LIFE, MOST IMPORTANTLY, IN SCHOOLS.

Subhadra and Ritika looked at each other and hugged each other in a long embrace.

HUMANITY
TRIUMPHS

HUMANITY TRIUMPHS

-Smita Potnis

(Translation from Hindi by - Anil Bapat / Dr Balaji Navale)

Smita Vijat Potnis is a Sci-Fi author with published stories in Marathi and Hindi. Her Sci-Fi stories have been included in a few books and articles on Sci-Fi and Science and have been printed in several regional magazines and newspapers. In addition to 'writing' science fiction stories, she has also written Sci-fi one-act plays, presented programs on Akashwani, and is also an active YouTube Creator via her channel "Marathi Sci-fi Stories Hub".

Outside Science fiction, Smita has also published other works including – My Nilangini - a novel concerning the story of Draupadi from Mahabharata, and a couple of religious books. Smita also enjoys writing and directing theatrical plays. Her one-act play won second prize in Avishkar one-act play competition.

Ramakant dropped an important message to the family to gather quickly. He noticed that the rest of the members had seen the message, so he started to get prepared himself.

You see, this was 2050. Now every family member had to have a separate room. It was mandatory and possible. It was mandatory, as virus outbreaks had become common, and when that occurred in any part of the world, all the family members needed to follow isolation, a kind of voluntary quarantine. The population of the world has diminished significantly since 2020. Governments had made it compulsory to construct large houses. It governed prices, buying and selling of houses, and indeed, it controlled the rest of the business and market activities. No one could disobey government order, public curfew, isolation, separation, lock-down and quarantine. Such isolation continued for up to six months or more than that. The virus COVID-21 has currently attacked the world. So, let's see what was happening in the family.

As Ramakant gears up for the meeting; Minal enters with breakfast dishes, hot coffee and fruits. Their daughter Juie and son Vijay, also enter the room.

"Iju, today there is your favourite cake."

"Mom, what is Iju? His name is Vijay. Viju is okay, but not Iju. He is grown up, and it is embarrassing", said Juie.

'Minal however stuck to her guns. Ramakant and she had fondly been calling the kids Juie and Iju, and the practice had continued. Minal ignored Juie's suggestion and invited both the children to enjoy breakfast.

"Papa, we didn't meet during the last two weeks. You imposed a strict rule: 'Don't come without a call' so we haven't come. But you did not tell us the reason, why so?" Juie asked Ramakant.

"Sorry, I know that you may have been upset about it. But let me clarify, I was in voluntary isolation, in quarantine in our own house."

"Why papa? Were you not feeling well? Juie exclaimed, "The virus must be shot dead with a big gun. How does it look, the virus"?

"All right. Of course, the virus has to be eliminated, but it is not that easy. We need to improve our immunity by taking preventive medicine and vaccines. The virus is a micro-atom not visible to our eyes. Then how can it be killed with a gun? The viruses are not even living things. In a virus, there aren't other atoms. It enters the human body, in our cells. It kind of overpowers the cells. Then such kind of controlled cells can't perform their duties. They only keep on generating a replica of the virus. Such infinite atoms are being produced continuously, till finally the cell breaks and the infinite virus atoms start spreading in our body," said Ramakant.

"But how does the virus reach us? Do they simply come walking to us?" On this innocent question of Iju, Ramakant just laughed and said, "They do not. We, humans, have a fancy for exploration. We explore wild birds and animals out of curiosity and even to satiate our appetite, which we should not. That is a route to viral infection. In mammal-like bats, there are 137 types of viruses. Among them, 61 types are harmful to human beings."

"Do the bats not get infected by so many viruses?" asked Juie.

'No, except by the rabies virus. But bats possess immunity to counterattack the rabies virus. Likewise, humans with strong immunity do not suffer much due to COVID-21 kind of viruses. Only the humans with weak immunity, like children and aged people, suffer more from such viral attacks", Ramakant clarified.

"Papa, why were you in self-quarantine in the house?" Juie asked.

Minal explained, "Juie, Karnik's uncle from the ground floor was ill. Papa went to take care of him. Don't worry, uncle did not have a viral infection. Poor fellow, he is aged and alone at home. He fell in his house and had a fracture. It was difficult for him to even get up from his bed. Who will visit him during the pandemic, as at present, when everyone is scared of the virus? He was weeping copiously on the phone when he called Papa. So, Papa went to his house, spent some time with him, consoled him, and returned after his uncle felt better. As a precaution, Papa stayed in isolation for two weeks, that was all".

"But why did you let him go? Had something happened to him?" Juie asked in anger. "Dear, Papa knew what he was up to. He took all precautions. He knows very well how dangerous the COVID-21 virus is. Out of concern for us, he observed isolation. Karnik's uncle was cured completely," explained Minal.

"But that was so unnecessary. I want you, Papa. Don't go to anyone," Juie would not let go of her grouse!

"Juie baby, nothing wrong happened to me" Papa consoled her, holding her close, and then, as if to take her mind off the topic, offered to tell a COVID virus tale, the usual lure used on kids to divert their minds!

She could not be fooled so easily. She was willing to hear the story, provided he promised that he would not go out again in such a situation.

Ramakant assured her that if, after hearing the story, she still insisted on a promise, he would make it. Juie nodded, and the story began.

The story was of the time when the COVID-19 virus attacked human beings all over the world, from the end of 2019. That virus attack created miserable conditions. Millions lost their lives, homes and means of livelihood. Migrant labour, hundreds of thousands of them, who were working in cities to earn a living, chose to walk back hundreds of kilometres to their villages. They quit the cities and the jobs, in the hope of being in their own homes, only to face ostracism when their weary legs took them to their native places. It was the time when not only the virus attack but also the migration and foolish behaviour of people resulted in the world population going down, while the politicians were at their usual game of one-upmanship and benefitting from the misery of others. This tale is of that time, Ramakant continued.

....

Rakhama was looking for any balance work to do in her house. There was nothing left to be done. But, staying idle was not an option. Gloomy thoughts were making her feel miserable. It was the house that used to host so many guests all the time. Both her kids used to be playing outside, creating a racket all the time. Rakhama was known for her kind heart, who would feed all neighbourhood kids when she fed her children. The neighbours used to admire her kindness and efficiency. In their opinion, she was the true mother of all children in the village. Those memories brought tears to her eyes. There was a time when she would continuously cater to guests and relatives at this very house. That would be physically tiring, but never once was her face without a welcoming smile. But in that very lively and big house, the three of them were now sitting inconspicuously, withdrawn into their shells. A thought crossed her sad mind, ever since the children had returned, they were not scattering around their things in their carefree manner anymore.

Her daughter Krushni was never interested in studies. Even her son Ramya had to be forced to sit down to study. They were now quietly reading their textbooks. Normally, they would want something to eat all the time, even after having meals. Not anymore, neither of them was asking for food. Rakhama observed in her mind, as she sat where the children were.

"Mummy, may I switch on the T.V.?" Krushni suddenly asked.

Rakhama was taken aback. "Switch on the TV? What will the people say?" she asked. "People? Which people?" Ramya asked.

"Our neighbours. They will say, you have lost your father, and you want to watch television?"

"Who is visiting us these days? In fact, now nobody visits anybody anymore" Krushni observed sullenly.

It was as if the raw scars on Rakhama's mind opened up and started bleeding. Twenty days from the sudden death of her husband, Vithoba, was hardly sufficient time for the scars to heal. As she performed his last rites all by herself over the next 13 days, the usually lively Rakhama had been dying an inward death in her mind. She was still not out of that frame of mind.

………………

The last time Vithoba returned from the city, he had found it to be gloomy and listless. His business required him to visit the city to sell his goods and to trade with Dharmeshbhai. This time when he returned home, he appeared tired and cheerless.

Rakhama asked him for the reason. She felt that maybe the absence of their children was the reason. So, she explained that the kids were excited when her brother came for a visit and chose to bunk the school to go and stay with him for a couple of weeks. She assured him that they would be back in two weeks and enquired as to why it took Vithoba longer this time to see Dharmeshbhai.

He replied that he did meet Dharmeshbhai, but that it was unlikely that he would be able to sell his goods this time around.

She expressed dismay. The crop had been abundant this time. The store was full and there was still the standing crop to be cut in the fields. She wondered if some other supplier was being preferred by Dharmeshbhai, over

Vithoba, this time. That would be unjust, she felt, as they were paying the agreed brokerage to Dharmeshbhai.

Vithoba was irritated. "Will you please keep quiet?" he said, "did I tell you that Dharmeshbhai has refused to do business with me?"

She persisted with the same line of thinking. "What then? Does he expect more commission?"

Vithoba was exasperated. "Dharmeshbhai lost his wife," he told Rakhama while signalling her not to pester him.

Rakhama was taken aback. She had questions about what happened to her, and whether she was ill when she died.

Vithoba gave her the details. Death had occurred when he was in the city. It was tragic what he saw, he told her. When Dharmeshbhai's wife passed away, her son and daughter-in-law did not even visit to see her one last time. Not only that, though they were staying in the deluxe flat purchased by Dharmeshbhai with his own money, the son had also asked him to stay at the bungalow in faraway Panvel, where there was no one to look after him. Vithoba wondered how Dharmeshbhai would manage in such a secluded place. Even the last rites had not been done for the departed person, he informed, just because the family did not want people to know. He said he had offered to bring Dharmeshbhai with him to his house, but that Dharmeshbhai declined, saying that what Vithoba had done for him, and his wife was more than enough. He had urged Vithoba to leave and return to his house, he said.

Rakhama was distressed. She was unable to make sense of what Vithoba was saying. "Tell me in detail, as you usually do. Do not avoid it just because it is painful" she urged.

"Even the memory is painful," he said. "But I shall not be comfortable if I hold it back from you. As per my usual practice, I went to Dharmeshbhai's house. He was not at home. I was told that he had gone to the hospital, as his wife was not well. His son and daughter-in-law were at home. They appeared to be a little scared. I thought it was natural. When his mother was hospitalized, the son was bound to be distressed. I am usually received very well in their house, but this time, it did not even strike the people in the house to take me in and offer me a glass of water. I was told in the door itself, that Dharmeshbhai had gone to the hospital. I was surprised. I asked his son, as to who was hospitalized and when was Dharmeshbhai expected to be back. The son informed me that he would not be returning so soon, as the mother was hospitalized. When I expressed shock and wanted to know more about it, the son was reluctant to speak normally. In a low voice, he urged me also to speak softly, as otherwise, they will have difficulty staying there".

Vithoba continued, "I felt slighted at such words of the son. I had not said anything wrong, that he should reply that way. But then, I said to myself that maybe his upbringing was not proper, he was not taught how to behave with guests. I asked for the name and address of the hospital and went there directly. After all, it cannot so happen that an acquaintance is in need in a hospital, and we do not go to him in his hour of need."

"When I reached there", Vithoba continued with his narration "I saw poor Dharmeshbhai was all alone and hungry. It was a government hospital. His wife was inside. He was asked to be outside. He said private hospitals had refused to admit her".

"Oh, my God!" Rakhama interrupted Vithoba. "Was she so seriously ill? But government hospital means rush, inconvenience and such things, as one hears. Is that true?" she asked.

"It is", he replied. "She was put on a stretcher, on the floor. There was a separate ward set up for patients suffering from the particular illness. She was having difficulty breathing. She should have been in an ICU, and on a ventilator. But ventilators were not available", he added.

"Oh no, what is this!" Rakhama exclaimed, "But isn't it that it is only when a patient is very serious that he is put on a ventilator?"

"Yes, you are right", he observed, "she had a high fever. Patients having difficulty in breathing have to be put on a ventilator. She was also having a dry cough. She had asthma too. Maybe these factors increased her illness. Doctors said she had that new virus infection, Coronavirus."

Rakhama recalled hearing the word Corona on TV several times, while she was busy cooking. In her simple manner, she had mistaken the term for Kareena Kapoor, the actress, thinking that it was some news related to her.

Vithoba explained to her that it was indeed an illness. He asked her if she knew about Chinese people, with their East Asian features, and habits like eating noodles. She replied in the affirmative, observing their habit of eating cockroaches, with some mirth. He continued to explain, that indeed those were the people and added that the disease was reported to have been transferred from the Chinese. He clarified that the Chinese used to eat any meat, raw and cooked, of any living creature imaginable. Whether fish or octopus snakes on land and in water. They are not averse to eating any creature. He added that the Chinese ate bats and that it had been reported that they were infected by the Coronavirus being carried by the bats. Dharmeshbhai had explained to him that a Chinese from a city called Wuhan was first infected by eating a live bat and that from him, the virus got transmitted to those around him.

Rakhama was repulsed. "What kind of people are they, eating bats!" she exclaimed. "Yes, this disease came from them. But then, who eats such things in Dharmeshbhai's house? God knows if his wife ate some Chinese dish and so got the disease. Whatever the reason, she suffered a lot due to the infection. Her stretcher was placed on a cold floor. All the money with Dharmeshbhai was of no use. Even her son did not visit her. His father could not go to his own house. He was so grateful that I visited him. He was completely shattered by the death of his wife. What good was having a son, if he was not there with him in the crisis? It was like his life as a human being was worthless, despite having so much wealth. There was no person to stand by him," Vithoba observed emotionally.

"It's not like that dear", consoled Rakhama, "it is destiny. It is karma. It is sad though. But could you then enquire elsewhere about selling our goods? When I called you, you said you were busy. Were you trying for another deal?"

He replied in the negative. He explained that none of the farmer producers will be able to get the services of middlemen, due to the Coronavirus pandemic. He indicated that he may have to organize delivery to the city or risk the produce going to waste.

Rakhama expressed faith in the God above. "He will bail us out", she said and inquired as to why was he late in returning.

Vithoba explained the plight of Dharmeshbhai, who was alone without any help. He said there was no help even to place the dead body of his wife in the hearse. Not even his son showed up. Vithoba explained that he helped Dharmeshbhai to take the dead body to the crematorium and to cremate her. That, he explained, was the reason why he returned late.

Rakhama was appreciative of his gesture. When she finished all the work and returned, she saw that Vithoba was already asleep.

The next day, Vithoba returned early from the farm. He said there was not much work to do at the farm. Even otherwise, he had a cold since he returned from the city. Now he had a cough too. When Rakhama enquired about it, he brushed it aside, saying it must be the hospital smells that gave him a cold.

His health continued to be the same for the next two days. He appeared to be tired. Rakhama got worried. She felt that the worries about selling the farm produce seemed to be bothering him. The issue was not yet resolved. It would be costly for Vithoba to cart his produce to the city alone. He was checking with a few others in the village to jointly transport their products, but nothing had worked out so far. She would wonder if he should be taking this to heart so much, as to fall ill. She would watch with concern that every day, he returned from the farm and went to sleep immediately. He was never so exhausted in the past. She wondered if she should call back the children to improve his mood.

The next day, when Rakhama had some free time for a change, she was watching T.V. All the channels were carrying stories about Coronavirus, and the destruction caused by the pandemic. She saw one expert advising against eating non-vegetarian food. Her family regularly ate chicken and mutton. In fact, like every time, Vithoba had carried a large quantity of fish from the city, which she had refrigerated and was included in every meal. She wondered if eating such food would affect the health of the family members. Another channel was giving information about the typical symptoms of the infection. The anchor explained that the infected person will have symptoms like cold and cough, breathing difficulty, diarrhoea, fever, and lung oedema. He added that the immunity of such an infected person would be affected. Rakhama was now carefully listening. The anchor went on to explain that the infection spread to a healthy person from an infected person, through sneezing and coughing by the latter and the droplets that flew on the body of the former as a result, or through touching an infected person. The virus lingered on articles touched by an infected person, he further explained and transmitted to a healthy person when he touched such articles later. The anchor stressed that the infection was spreading like wildfire, and therefore, he urged the listeners to take all due precautions. The saving grace, he said, was that the infected persons did get cured, provided they received treatment in time. He advised that persons having any of the symptoms must rush to a hospital and do a COVID-19 test. If the test is positive, the person must get admitted immediately. The distance must be maintained by healthy persons, from the infected ones, he concluded. Rakhama was listening intently to all that the anchor was saying. She was convinced by what she heard.

Suddenly she realized that Vithoba had carried the body of Dharmeshbhai's wife, who was infected and who had died of Coronavirus and had performed her last rites. She visualized what may have happened, and shuddered. "He touched her body, carried it. Did he touch his face and nose with the same hands?" The very thought put a shiver through her spine. She consoled herself, that all this hearsay may not be true. She felt the channels were fearmongering. "How can an act of humanity and compassion result in infection, it cannot be! she reasoned to herself.

On that very day, Vithoba returned from the farm panting. She realized that his symptoms were not good. She touched him and found that he had a high fever. He went to bed, even as she offered food, which he declined. She suggested that they go to the doctor, but he declined, saying that he had no energy and that they could visit the doctor the next day. She even offered to call the doctor home. But he would not have it. He then went to sleep, but after some time he woke up, breathless. Rakhama was scared. She rushed to her neighbour, Appa Patil, for help. Appa told her that the doctor was not in the village that day, so she would have to wait for a day.

At Appa's place, she also saw the announcement of lockdown from midnight. That was shocking. The instructions during lockdown were for all to stay in their houses, not to venture out. Wear a mask. Keep a meter's distance. Not to visit anyone. Tears started running down her eyes, even as she suddenly realized that she was in her neighbour's house. As she rushed back running from there, it did not escape her notice that no one asked her to be with them to regain her composure.

The first thing she did was to call her brother on the phone and tell him all these developments while sobbing relentlessly.

Her brother told her that he would not like to bring the children back immediately, as then he too would be stuck in her house. His wife and kids would then be left alone. He assured her that the children were comfortable there and that she should not worry about them. He assured her that Daji, meaning Vithoba, would be alright. He advised her to take care of Vithoba as well as herself. He promised to send the children back in the police officer's van, when possible. She started crying. There was nobody around to help. Her children were not with her. She didn't know what to do.

She looked after Vithoba while taking all precautions for herself. The doctor did not return to the village. Vithoba did not receive any medical help. There was no vehicle available to take him to the hospital. She was doing whatever best she could. She tried to maintain his morale. However, in the end, Vithoba could not sustain himself. One night, he passed away quietly, without disturbing her. She did not even realize when he died. He was keen to see his children one last time, but, as if realizing the risk, he had told her not to bring them back any too soon. When she found out he had died, she just could not control her grief.

Dharmeshbhai's son refused to see his dying mother. Vithoba, who was dying, kept his children safely away, out of his affection for them. The contradiction hit her hard. Why should things happen this way! She wailed and started weeping loudly. In the quiet of the dawn, the wails surely reached the doors of many in the village, but they did not reach the ears of those inside. Fear of Corona froze the sound of the wails at the doorsteps!

She waited to see if someone had come around to enquire. Nobody turned up, not a soul! It was such a cruel fate for her husband, who used to help everyone, to die all alone, as if not cared for by anybody! What sort of justice was this, her heart screamed. She wept long and hard, and with strong feelings. Then she controlled her emotions. There was a wooden plank lying in the backyard. She brought it in. She covered her body in a plastic sheet and tied a cloth around her face. With a steely resolve, she pushed Vithoba's dead body onto the plank. She pulled the plank all the way to the crematorium. She did not come across any policemen enforcing the lockdown. A few people saw her passing through the road, from the safety of their homes. But no one came outside to help her. Even as she wept all the way, her mind was becoming numb and emotionless. Her tears dried up, by the time she reached the crematorium. She was exhausted by the effort, breathing laboriously. She collected the pyre woods lying around. She arranged the pyre. She had great difficulty placing Vithoba's body on top of the pyre. But she did it. She lit the pyre with the torch that was there, chanting the names of the gods. Vithoba was punished by COVID-19 for showing humanity. She threw the plastic sheet used by her to cover her body, in the same pyre, as if to destroy the virus that may be clinging on the sheet.

....

There was nobody at home to insist that she eat something. She took an elaborate bath, rubbing her body vigorously with soap. No one was there to offer her food, nor did she have any appetite. She washed the whole house. Vithoba was not used to doing any housework, Rakhama would provide him with whatever he wanted. She had pampered him, spoilt him. During the last sickness, she was cautious enough to wrap plastic around her palms, like protective gloves. She used to wear a separate gown while nursing him, which would be separately washed. All her precautions now culminated in washing the whole house.

Despite such precautions, no Pundit was willing to do the final rites of Vithoba in her house. No one visited. With folded hands, she prayed to the Gods and the departed soul of her husband, wishing it everlasting peace, freedom, and salvation.

She narrated her plight to her brother, in a matter-of-fact manner, without crying. He too was not able to come due to the lockdown. He requested the police officer in the area for help. The officer told him that Rakhama had done the last rites of her husband. He advised waiting for 14 days, just to ensure that she was not infected and promised that thereafter he would reach the children in his van.

When her brother explained these developments to her, she agreed. Now she had become stoic just like a saint. She agreed with the logic of the police officer's suggestions. After a fortnight, her children returned. Nobody else visited, though she was not infected.

Children returned, but they had withdrawn into shells. It was not as if their father used to be at home with them all the time. But he was there earlier, and now it was clear that he would never return. That awareness had made them numb, speechless.

Rakhama offered them an emotional release. "Ramya, Krushni, come to me and feel free to weep," she told them. They hugged her tight and wept their hearts out.

Then she got up. She offered fresh and hot food to the children, and she also had some.

....

It was now 20 days after Vithoba's death. Rakhama felt that the children were right. There had been no visitors to their house in the last 20 days. So, who would visit, and who would blame them, if the television set was switched on! She switched the TV on and joined the children in watching.

The newsreader was informed that COVID-19 was the 19th version of the original Coronavirus. She added that ten new viruses were reportedly identified in addition to COVID-19. Rakhama wondered to herself if this was like the reincarnation of Gods in Hindu mythology. Her children couldn't but smile at the simile.

The newsreader continued "Viruses resulting in running noses in infected persons are known as rhinoviruses, that is, viruses that proliferate in the nose. Rhino means nose. Rhinoceros means an animal with a horn on its snout". She went on to inform that when, in the initial phase, the Coronavirus was transmitted from bats to humans, it caused a lot of many deaths of humans.

"Your father had told me that the virus had originated from the bats", she informed the children, even as she continued to view the TV with interest.

The newsreader then presented a new angle to look at the issue. She spoke about the impact of the pandemic on the environment. She pointed out that the authorities directed the shutting down of factories and offices and instead to work from home. That resulted not only in reduced use of power, and therefore of fuel, but the emission of various toxic gases also reduced as a result, she said. There was an improvement in the air quality of polluted cities, greenhouse gases had gone down, Ozone depletion had been arrested, and rivers were getting cleaner, she added. She informed me that prior to the pandemic, many efforts had been made to purify the Ganges, which had not yielded much. However, she added, that the lockdown prevented the infusion of poisonous chemicals, dead bodies, animal parts, excreta and gutter water, old clothing, garbage, ashes immersed by relatives during the last rites of the dead, and thereby cleaning up the Ganges corridor. The water appears transparent now, she said. Rakhama was amazed to learn about these changes. When she saw the images of the holy Ganges, she bowed in reverence as a devout Hindu who considers the Ganges her mother.

She recalled her guilt at not being able to immerse Vithoba's ashes in the Ganges, which was believed to result in the salvation of the soul of the departed person. She had wept at that time. But now here was a new perspective. The river gets polluted by such immersion. Suddenly her guilt at being unable to carry out the last rites of Vithoba in the traditional manner disappeared. She realized that it contaminated the environment, and in return, human beings ultimately suffered. Now that the humans were prevented from going on with such destructive rituals and practices, nature seemed to be rejuvenating.

Just then Ramya observed, that if all had to stay at home, then he need not go to school. His sister pointed out that it would simply be sitting at home, day after day. No friends to play with within the compound or even at home. Ramya was not ready for that. But he was scared too. "Will I die if I go out?" he asked. Rakhama pulled him close. "Don't be silly", she said.

Krushni had a question for her mother. She wondered as to why human beings had been singled out to suffer the virus when they too were a part of nature. That got Rakhama thinking. She remembered Vithoba, and her eyes welled up.

She started wondering if it was because the population had exploded. She remembered a TV program which had shown the tendency in some species of animals that if their number increased, the elder among them jumped to death from atop the hills, to control the population. Human beings never took any such step, they just fought each other as monkeys did. She wondered therefore if it was nature's way of reducing the number of humans living on the earth.

As the children were talking to her and among themselves, Rakhama switched off the TV. She asked them to be quiet. Just as she said that there was a shrill wail emanating from Appa Patil's house, which penetrated her door frame and entered her house. She was startled. Patil's wife was talking about his death. "O, God!" Rakhama said to herself "What should I do now? Should I go to her for help? But then, where did they come to my help?" Corona had cursed and cut out all compassion in humans. Rakhama was now the only parent to her children. So, what was she to do? Rakhama was in two minds. If the neighbours had erred in not coming to her help, should she repeat the mistake? Was that in order? But then what about humanity? If one human did not help another, who else will? Compassion towards other human beings was natural. One may take precautions. Like how the doctors do. Had a doctor been available, Vithoba could have been saved. But protecting the body does not mean shutting the mind to the misery of others. The mind has to be open. Minds must meet. If you help someone now, that person may help you in your hour of need. In a society, rather, than in nature itself, all were interdependent. Tomorrow, she may need help with farming. Human beings had to stand by each other. Such were the thoughts that raced through her mind.

She was sure that nobody else would venture out of their homes. She was aware of how Patil's wife would be feeling at that point in time. She was aged and alone, both her grown-up sons were away in the city. They would not be able to come. Should she go to her help? The COVID-

19 virus was here to divide humanity. But while keeping a distance from each other, the minds too were becoming distant, humanity was being destroyed. Rakhama had experienced the non-cooperation in her hour of need. She, therefore, knew exactly how much help was essential. Who else would know that better than her?

She got up. She had already fed her children. The wailing of Patil's wife had scared them a lot. Rakhma told them in a firm voice, that she would go to help the neighbour, and that should the children feel hungry, there was food available at home. She told them that the neighbour needed help.

"But, Mummy, what if you get infected! Daddy suffered a curse, simply because he went to help someone," the children protested.

She asked them not to be worried. She explained that nothing would happen to her if she took precautions. She told them that Vithoba was ignorant about taking precautions. She explained to them that nothing happened to her despite nursing Vithoba, as she had done that carefully. "Coronavirus is testing humanity. It checks if we maintain personal hygiene. If we do that, the virus gets eliminated. Do understand that. I need to go and help. Please do not worry", she said.

Then she wore her face mask, wrapped the plastic sheet, and with such due precautions, she set out of her house, to uphold the code of humanity.

……………………..

Ramakant ended the story and then asked. "Juie, tell me now. An animal, a bird, or for that matter, even a virus does not change its nature and function. Should then humans forget humanity? If yes, then how can we be called human beings?"

"Papa, was that a real story, or did you make it up?" Juie asked. "Of course, it was a true story" Papa assured, "it is the story of my mummy, your grandmother. I am Ramya in the story. Now tell me, should or shouldn't have I gone to help Karnik uncle?" He asked.

The doting daughter that she was, Juie replied as only she could. "Yes, you should have. But in future, you won't go. I shall, like my granny", she told him, even as she hugged him fondly. Ramakant held her close, even as he laughed at her answer.

As luck would have it, the health minister of India went on air at that very moment to announce that a vaccine had been successfully tested against COVID-21 and that India would not patent it, but allow it to be mass-produced and sold cheap, for the sake of entire mankind! Humanity scored again!!

....

So, you see! The year does not matter, whether 2020 or the present, 2050. Students then used to go to school. Now they learn from home. But it is still one of the functions of the parents to inculcate values in their children. Let it be any virus. We, the humans, should guard ourselves against it, but we should not give up on the values of humanity and compassion.

Stay home, keep distance, stay safe but don't forget humanity.

MAZDUR DHABA

MAZDUR DHABA

-Sourav Ghosh

Sourav Ghosh is a writer and a translator. He studied Electronics & Communication Engineering (ECE) at SRM University, Chennai. Also, he has studied Spanish language at CUI- Centro Universitario de Idiomas, Argentina. He hails from Kolkata, West Bengal. He has written several short stories and published a few books. As a translator, he has translated Spanish stories including science fiction in Bengali. Currently, He is working as a data scientist at Boeing Aerospace.

Village Charida, Purulia, West Bengal April 2020:

Little Nitu immersed another layer of paper in diluted glue. During this emergency period, a child at her age should care about online classes whereas she has to care about filling her stomach. The more number of masks she can prepare and sell, the more money she can earn for her daily bread. There is no difference between a national emergency and other days for her family. She knows the struggle is another name for life. Rather than the COVID-19 crisis, the financial crisis stained their birth rights long before. In Charida they are not very much literate enough to know the name of the virus or the root cause of the pandemic. They only know Death came in disguise as the deadly disease to abolish humanity from the planet. 'The curse of Mahakal'- Grandma used to nod and speak. Nitu remembered.

Till now there have been skeletons of ten facial Masks she has prepared. She counted carefully. A special layer of mud and cloth is already applied to them and then these masks will be sun-dried. Nitu and her family are from the sutradhar community. Twenty-five families are struggling across Charida in the same community. Nitu's family one among them, used to prepare chhau masks for chhau dance. Chhau dance is a famous ritualistic approach in Bengal, performed during the spring festival of Chaitra Parva. The traditional dance is based on a choreographic explanation of Indian mythical characters depicted in ancient pieces. To characterize individuals, artists wear colourful traditional masks with aesthetic designs. This festival had a great tourist value which strengthened the state's economy. But now COVID-19 world pandemic destroyed all the resources.

The business of chhau masks has been barred since then. This barbaric disease has taken the lives of many but could not take away hunger, and poverty from the community families. To support their existence, the community started making facial masks the same way they used to make chhau masks. They go to the city by cycle daily basis and sell as much as they can. Though Nitu's family had a side income, right now that's also not guaranteed. Nitu's father works as a building construction labour during the off-season of chhau musk production.

One month back he got a labour contract and left for the city pouring lots of hopes in his eyes. Lots of dreams to be taken care of lots of promises to be filled for his only child. Even last week also father and daughter had a long discussion over the phone. He was on the way to coming back to his village. But now everything is lost. "Lockdown" for an indefinite time ruined the whole plan. Nitu tried to reach her father, but the phone was switched off.

--" Nitu Ma...Is Moloy at home?", Laxmi Dadi asked. She is an old lady from Nitu's neighbour. Her son Prabir is a friend of Nitu's father, Moloy.

-- "No Dadi", Nitu replied.

-- "Oh! Here it if. You see. I came here to say that a group of people came by car to provide relief." Dadi continued her speech. She put a longleaf tied to her face just like facial musk." They said they are here to help. Later they blabbered something which I could not understand.

When I asked them where they were coming from? some phrase they said 'Korana'. I never heard such a village name in the neighbourhood."

National Institute of bioresearch & diseases Kolkata, West Bengal

April 2020:

-- " Can you tell me the location again...Mashud's Dhaba right? "

--" No chief it's 'Mazdur'...means labour class people.", Akash answered it quickly, like an obedient student. He stumbled upon the classified test reports from that location which he is carrying now. With the flow of time, he may forget his identity but "Mazdur Dhaba", that geo-location tag will never fade away from his memory.

Dr Dinesh Kumaran, with experience of 32 years in virology, is the current chief of COVID-19 test procurement in the Bengal region. Prof. Akash Mitra, a young blood, is working under him, leading the team wholeheartedly to fight this pandemic. But recently while surging the COVID test campaign at a state highway near Purulia city they have found few test reports are extremely unexpected.

The government had to carry forward the tests as the gathering of labour-class people was high in a few dhabas. These shocking results created a wave of excitement across the team. It's a strange notion of light in this dark period. Even Dr Kumaran never believed it at first sight.

-- "Is there any positive case from that Dhaba? "

-- No chief.

-- " So, do you still want to keep this result as classified? This is of course news. The world must know this breakthrough...!" Kumaran said, tipping off his face mask gently over the nose.

-- " I did not announce this in press conference yet.", Akash nodded. "I think we need more time to investigate further. We also need more test samples. Twelve samples are not enough to rush for statistical confirmation. "

-- " I see! Do you think it's a strategic human trial without making social awareness? Dr Kumaran smiled. "You know Akash, labourers are always guinea pigs of any social experiments. Whether it's a trade war or a biological traumatized issue, in the end, it's them...only them. We let them run in the wheel of life keeping food and money as bait. Based on their survival rate we analyse the disaster. heh!" The devil inside Kumaran just smilingly spoke the truth.

-- " Maybe a mass human trial it was. But the only question that has been tickling my mind since the day I analysed this report. Whoever started this trial -Who are they and what they are developing underneath? "

Akash and Kumaran stared at each other for an instant. They can't sense the mystery. Their vision is blurred.

-- " Anyway, we are far away from our target Akash. Use your whole damn resource & finish off the job. Gather a sufficient amount of plasma in whichever way you can... " Dr Kumaran broke the silence to ease the discussion.

-- "And after that...?"

-- " After that what?! Let them free...Do you know what this means...?"

-- " No Sir.", Akash could not overcome his anxiety. But inside he started realizing something worse was going to happen.

-- " Give them food and money. release them. Make them happy. That's it! Now finish this off quickly. we have lots to work on in a short time." Kumaran said loud and clear.

-- "And chief what about the origin of this...?"

-- "I don't care."

-- "But there are around 80 subjects and we do not have much time on our hands. Only 6 days! Only 6 days more in our camp can survive there.", Akash requested effortlessly.

--" See son...never get dependable on the requirement. Be the requirement. So, do it now and make this country proud." Kumaran signed off the meeting.

Mazdur Dhaba, State Highway, Purulia, West Bengal April 2020:

Due to the lockdown, there is no transport available between Purulia city and village. Previously there were connecting buses from city to village but now everything is closed. Like other labourers, Moloy was also walking towards the village taking the road trip. They were a group of five members, Moloy and Junaid's family. Moloy and Junaid were from the same village, Charita. They met at the construction site and became friends. Junaid was having a 6-year-old boy and a 9-year-old girl. Both of them were so exhausted that they slept on the luggage. One was getting dragged by Junaid and the other one by his wife. there was a gushing sound coming out from that little girl. Her thin chappal is yet to be torn apart into pieces. It might be exhausted just like her. Moloy observed due to hunger the drop of her saliva was secreting out from her mouth. Her red colour facial musk was getting wet and more reddish, looked like old bloodstained. Moloy felt sorry. He started thinking about his lovely daughter. Nitu will be almost the same age as Junaid's daughter. Maybe 3-4 years older than her. Moloy asked himself. What would she be doing now at home? Maybe struggling alone? There is no way to reach her because Moloy's mobile battery drained out just like Junaid's phone.

After walking a few more kilometres some ray of hope flashed in their eyes. There's a Dhaba nearby. A big signboard in Red and yellow hanging from the top "Mazdur Dhaba (Rs 1/- per meal)". It was medium crowded. They all were probably a group of labourers similar to Moloy's group. Far away from their home, they were taking refuge here in Dhaba. Their eyes were looking for food while they gave rest to their tired limbs.

In one corner of Dhaba, there was a small standing placard. "Prasad from the nearby temple" is written on it in Bengali. Below that, There were three trays full of Bundi. Needless to say, those were free of cost. Most of the guests are taking a handful of Bundi from there. As the hunger strived hard, there was no bar of caste and creed in front of hunger. They believed the Supreme was one in this catastrophe. Moloy and Junaid also didn't leave this opportunity. Junaid shared the sweet with his family. This little sweet put glee on their pale, hungry faces. As a flow of time crowd and fear started getting increased. They ordered food.

Suddenly there's a sound came. A car has been parked outside the Dhaba premises. few people went out to see it. Panic has stricken on everyone's face.

Media and reporters were covering the story. In Mazdur Dhaba as the gathering of labour class people was huge there has been live broadcast of this news drawing a comparison with Tablighi-Nizamuddin Jamaat. Immediately police reached over the spot and took the charges. The whole Dhaba was shut down and sealed. People inside it were also quarantined. To handle the situation with ease Police brought UV-Bluster to sanitize the whole area. The UV blusters are human-friendly and effective to disinfect a large area rapidly. Each bluster consists of 6 UV bulbs of 43 watts, which in total have a radiation wavelength of 254 nm. Fear and rumour spread more like wildfire among innocent quarantined labourers when a medical team was sent by the government to test COVID. Among the masses, few said that the team came to diagnose them as all of them were already infected with the disease. "Death is near" They all stitched that idea with their mind and soul.

National Institute of bioresearch & diseases Kolkata, West Bengal, April 2020:

-- " So, what's the current progress of test? ", Kumaran asked anxiously.

Akash smiled, "As I said chief the time is very much limited but still, we progressed our research within these 4 days. Till now we have tested 55 plasma samples following a monoclonal antibody search. We are close enough to say the gathering was a human trial. We can guarantee that we can get 10 more samples from there. Then the test ratio will complete to hundred per cent"

-- " I see. interesting! And which method did you follow? Same as gene editing test-principal? ", Kumaran is excited. He put off his glasses on the table.

-- " Yes sir.", Akash smiled again." We believe some kind of vaccine has been injected or fed in the subject's body might be via food or some other means, which is acting as a strong combined effect of B38 and H4 neutralizing antibodies somehow.

Whereas right now our global research could think of rational vaccine design following the trade of these two antibodies."

-- "Of. Go on."

-- " The case triggered me more when I found zero positive cases from the mass at the beginning. The reports were totally clean. After that one result came positive in the first round of tests and negative in the second round with a gap of just 6 hours. With this great variance at first, we thought our test kit had some faults. But afterwards, this variation started increasing in the blink of an eye. As you know most of the migrant labourers in that gathering came from different red zone areas."

-- " I see..."

-- " Even after that we dug deep. We put our whole effort into finding out whether they have ever been a victim of COVID-19 or not. While investigating that we discovered the working principle of this vaccine. In 6 hours between the gap of the first round and second round of tests, they were getting the vaccine. We did not know the source until then."

-- That is totally strange.

-- Yes, chief absolutely! Wait the picture is not yet finished here..., Akash smiled.

-- Go on...Go on...

-- When we investigated further, we found in that Dhaba nothing except a tray of Bundi as prasad, nothing left. When we brought a few samples from there and tested them, we were in deep shock.

-- So, you found it?

-- Yes chief… But there is some strange behaviour it is showing rather than what is expected. I think we need to run more tests on that.

-- Ok… explain...

-- As per expectation when both the antibodies are putting their combined effect, they first deactivate the protein spike of SARS-CoV-2. This bans the virus from attaching to ACE-2 receptors in human cells so that the virus will never get a chance to infect. But there is a high chance that the virus will evolve with genetic mutation and fight back being stronger than last time. Here comes the working of this vaccine in effect like a double-edged sword. It banns the evolution of the virus and slows poison its life cycle which slowly leads to the destruction of this evil.

-- That's pretty strange. Now I am eager to know the origin. A great trial indeed.

-- Yes chief.

They both smiled.

-- So, Press conference? Kumaran asked.

-- Not yet chief!

-- Good! Be sharp and make it quick.

State Highway, Purulia, West Bengal April 2020:

--" Junaid... Junaid", Moloy whispered. " Are you awake?"

Junaid blinked. The past two days they were planning for this opportunity. Moloy has to reach Nitu whatever it costs. Deep inside he knows not this deadly disease, if something can kill him, it will be poverty. His life is not very valuable, but Nitu's is. She should live.

-- " Junaid we will not take the highway anymore. Do you listen? We will follow the railway tracks and finally reach our destination."

Junaid agreed. They have to reach by any means. The night is gloomy and silent. They left the Dhaba silently. Everyone was in deep sleep. Junaid and Raziya, holding their children. Moloy was leading them. Moloy could manage to charge his mobile for 5 minutes. He saw a two per cent charge left on his mobile. The time is midnight. He should call Nitu to inform him that he is coming. He is coming at last. A new red dress for her, new toys from the city everything is resonating from his bag pack. His mind and body are fighting against all his fear. There was only sound he could hear "Need to reach...need to reach" There was a light and a whistle they all could feel. It's coming. it's coming like a fireball in the dark. maybe a time tunnel is taking them right now to help them reach the destination quickly...whatever it is, in the end, they are tired. They are standing still, ready to be taken away.

***

Nitu woke up. That was a really bad dream. A nightmare which she never wanted to see anymore. She will wait until her father arrives. She never believes in the curse of Mahakal. She believes neither in deadly diseases nor any vaccine. She only knows that to discover the vaccine of poverty it will take much longer.

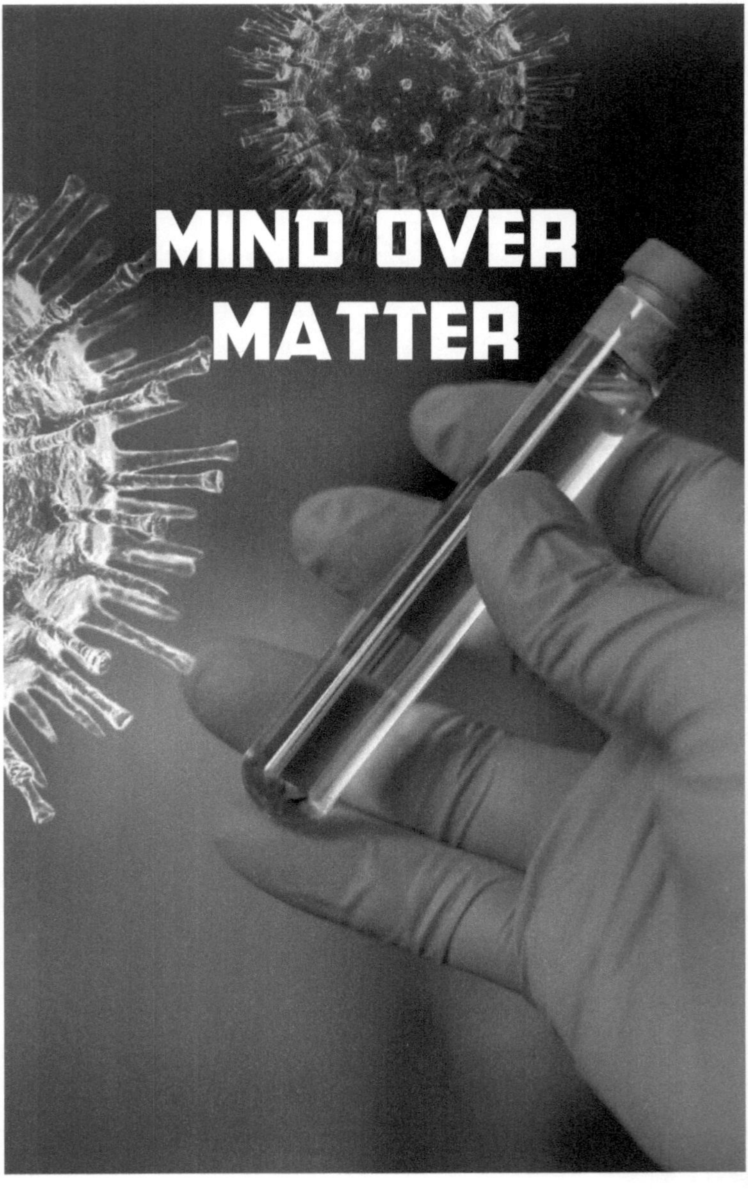
MIND OVER
MATTER

MIND OVER MATTER

-Archana Mirajkar

Archana Mirajkar is an author who writes in English and Marathi. Her books include 'All the Way… Home' (a science fiction novel), 'Swayamsiddha' (a collection of stories based on rebellious characters from Mahabharat), and 'Hello, kon?' (a two-act play). She has translated many distinguished authors from English into Marathi. Her YouTube series 'Granthyatra' showcases a hundred outstanding books in Marathi literature. Archana has worked as a communications specialist and journalist for 26 years. Currently, she is a Senior Media and Communications Officer at a foreign mission in Delhi.

Gayatri's back ached. She had been sitting on her stool, hunched over the eyepiece of her microscope for a long time. Sample after sample that she had examined for the past more than two hours had shown the growth of the virus. Not a single drug mixed in those cultures had been able to kill it. Yes, some cultures did show weak growth, but the unmistakable trace of the virus was always there.

Gayatri began to feel very uneasy. The import was serious. None of the drugs that were in the trials were succeeding against the virus. All the drug combinations allotted to her group had failed.

Meanwhile, people were dying by the thousand. The delay of every single day in finding the cure was devastating hundreds of families.

Gayatri got up from her seat and decided to take a coffee break. It meant removing the personal protection attire that she wore above her normal clothes from head to toe. She would then have to go to the scrubbing room and scrub her hands thoroughly. Crossing several electronically locked doors, she will have to exit the laboratory building and then cross over to the common area and enter the cafeteria. Then follow all the same procedures in reverse order to get back to work. The protocol was not only cumbersome but also time-consuming, so Gayatri often skipped her meals. Time was crucial and she somehow felt that every moment she wasted, took a human life somewhere on the planet.

When she entered, the cafeteria was deserted. Even until six months ago, she would have waged anything to find a quiet moment to sit down with her coffee. The cafeteria was always full of people and buzzing with conversations and laughter twenty-four hours a day. People worked in shifts at the biggest pharma company in New York. But the virus came and all that changed. Most people now worked from home and researchers like her worked in isolated labs with minimal contact with other workers. Despite Gayatri's disposition for solitude, the silence in the cafeteria seemed eerie.

As Gayatri sat at a corner table sipping her coffee, her mind continued to work on the drug combinations. All the drugs that had shown potential in the initial phase of the viral infection were now failing. Why this should be the case was baffling. When one of the companies at the forefront of the anti-COVID research announced a successful combination of drugs against the virus, it was deployed in a particular state of the US on a trial basis. When that state showed positive results and the deaths dropped dramatically, the drug was approved for use in other states. But within a week or so, it would turn out to be ineffective. In two or three weeks, the drug would completely fail to cure even a single case of the viral infection. The scientist would then have to go back to their drawing board.

The drug combination that Gayatri was presently working with was touted as the 'wonder drug' just last month. After successfully treating twenty thousand patients in the first week, it began to fail in other states. The company then asked Gayatri and her team to try a few modifications of the combination of the virus. That is what Gayatri was engaged with for the past week. And today, when she tested the twelve different combinations that she had injected into the virus cultures in her lab, she found none of them to be effective against the growth of the virus.

Gayatri was not just disappointed… she was stunned and furious. There has to be a way to kill the virus… They would have to find a solution. She had to succeed. She had to find a cure. And there was no time to waste. Gayatri gulped down the remaining coffee in her mug and dashed back to her laboratory.

………………………………

Sandhya slowly closed the door of her bedroom, carefully avoiding any noise, and tiptoed to her workstation. She had just fed her infant daughter and as soon as the child had dozed off, Sandhya tucked her comfortably with a blanket and got back to her work. The 4:00 PM deadline was approaching, and she had to send the final data to the control room. The spokesperson of the Health Ministry would need the latest figures for the evening press briefing.

Sandhya began where she had left half an hour ago and her fingers moved deftly on the keypad of her

laptop. Another huge spike in the cases…. the largest in a day so far….and yet another peak in deaths. New infections in areas that had been declared safe…. more areas sealed and more people quarantined. The news was as bleak as it could get.

Sandhya was scared. What kind of world would her daughter grow in? When was this pandemic going to end? She brushed aside the thought and concentrated on the task at hand. After she had sent the latest figures to the ministry control room, she turned to another set of figures she had to send to a pharma company in the US. The data compilation company that Sandhya worked for had several high-profile clients and it was Sandhya's job to dispatch the custom-made reports to most of these clients.

She was good at her work, but this was not how she had dreamed about her post-maternity leave work. She had imagined it would be a gradual transition, with a few hours in the beginning and returning to full-time work only when her daughter was at least a year old. After all, she deserved time off from work as she had worked until the last day before she gave birth to her daughter. Her company had to develop the contact tracing app and she had agreed to lead the team to meet the deadline. When she had signed off on that project, just a day before getting admitted to the hospital for her daughter's birth, she had imagined the pandemic would be a thing of the past before she resumed work.

But things had changed rapidly. Within five months of her daughter's birth, the pandemic had wreaked havoc across the country, forcing a strict lockdown. Everyone was confined to their homes and everything except the most essential services had shut down. Every day, more and more people turned up at the hospital and the number of casualties began to build up. Sandhya's company called her and requested her to join work from home. Sandhya agreed because by now, fear had possessed her too. She was afraid for the safety of her family and would rather know what was going on than hear the half-truths parading as news on social media.

And what she had learnt in this one month since resuming her work was frightening. The more the administration fought the spread of the disease, the more it came back with a resurgence. If one area was sealed, it appeared in another area. When that area was locked down, it appeared in some other area hitherto declared safe. Whatever the health professionals or the administrators tried, the virus was always one step ahead…

The phone rang and Sandhya came out of her reverie with a jerk… "Hello!" she said, answering the phone.

"Hi, Sandhya! This is Gayatri from NewMed Pharma. I haven't received the data from India yet, so just wanted to check…"

"Hi! Yes, it is ready. Sorry, it got delayed. Will send you in a minute…"

The two women had gotten to know each other quite well over the past month as they often chatted about the implications of their work and speculated on the possible course of the pandemic.

"Any breakthrough Gayatri?" Sandhya asked hopefully.

"None. This virus defies me. Nothing seems to work against it…" "That's bad… I am afraid!"

"I am afraid too…"

"What's the news on your side?"

"The numbers are going up, as always. There's no flattening the curve." "Hmm. and pattern? What about the pattern?"

"Aggressively spreading to new areas… It is as if. as if…"
"As if what?"

"No no. You will think I am mad." "Tell me. What are you thinking?'

"It is as if the virus has a mind of its own… it understands what we are doing, and counteracts…" "Well, it's only a virus. A virus can't have a mind…"

………………………………

Gayatri parked her car at the curb and looked across the street towards the house on the opposite side. It looked like any ordinary house, but she knew that it housed an extraordinary individual… Professor David Boyle. Gayatri took a deep breath, gathered her courage and getting out of the car, strode towards the entrance of the house. When she rang the doorbell, the professor answered it himself.

He looked just as he did on TV shows… old, unsteady and a little grumpy. "Good evening, Professor Boyle. I am Gayatri," she said.

The professor turned inwards, and Gayatri followed hesitantly him into his house. The professor took a seat in the hallway and gestured for her to be seated. She sat at a respectable two feet distance from him.

"I can't thank you enough professor for agreeing to meet me…" she began.

The professor dismissed her small talk with a wave of his hand and asked her abruptly: "What did you wish to discuss with me?"

"All the drug combinations we have tried are failing against coronavirus. Even those that are effective initially, lose out in a week or two."

"Some viruses mutate… that's their natural coping mechanism… But I'm not a virologist. How can I help you?" asked the professor peering at her above the rim of his glasses.

"I know professor. But I think we are using the wrong technique to beat this virus. And I have a hypothesis whose plausibility I want to check with you before I propose it to the management of my company."

"Go on…"

"Professor, I have been a fan of your writings and I have learnt a lot about the latest research in the intersecting field of biology and physics through your books. Your theory of blocks of rudimentary consciousness at the particle level has fascinated me. I was wondering… if… if this virus has a mind of its own." Gayatri blurted out what she wanted to say before her logical mind could blow holes in her theory.

The professor chuckled and began to shake his head.

"It doesn't work that way. I never said viruses are conscious…"

"No no, I don't mean it that way. But all the data points to the fact that the virus is always one step ahead of whatever measures we adopt to stop its spread. I know mutations are a natural phenomenon but the speed at which this virus wriggles out of every trap is astonishing. Professor, I have been working on the drug combinations to kill this virus for the past six months. I have been analysing the data of its behaviour, not just here in the US but in several countries across all continents. And I am convinced, this virus is actively working to counter the measures taken against it. Despite there being no contact between two patients, it adopts defensive mechanisms to counter a drug being administered to one patient before it is introduced in the other." Gayatri noticed that the professor was no longer shaking his head but was listening to her attentively.

"What's more, the virus sometimes anticipates our next move and begins to build defences against it. I am scared professor… very very scared. I don't see how the viruses can communicate with each other without being in physical contact with each other…"

"It's possible!"

Gayatri almost choked! The professor was confirming her worst fears.

"How?"

"It's not been proved yet but primitive life forms such as viruses could have particle entanglement. It is now well known that viruses communicate with each other by releasing messenger molecules in the host organism. Through these messages, the viruses collectively decide whether to go for a burst of replications and thereby kill the host or to lay dormant and wait for a more suitable time.

It is possible that when the viruses jump from one host to another, they release messenger molecules in the new host; each of which has a particle entanglement with the messenger molecules released in the previous host. Now whenever the environment in the new host changes and the viruses release more communication particles, similar changes occur in the communication particles circulating through the previous host. The viruses present in the previous host read these changes in the communication molecules and decide their strategy. And when they jump to yet another host, they carry these altered communication molecules to that host. And so on…."

"This is very scary. The viruses are smarter than us!" Gayatri couldn't believe what she was hearing. "I wouldn't say that", said Professor Boyle. "Viruses can communicate but they are not conscious like humans."

"What's the difference?" asked Gayatri.

"What it means is that most of this communication occurs at a subconscious level. The viruses are not aware that they are individuals distinct from their host, say humans. Or that they are intentionally devising schemes to kill the human race. Their communication is a survival instinct. They are perhaps communicating if the theory can be proved, but merely to survive and propagate."

"Professor, you should be at the forefront of the battle against COVID. You should be leading the research to find a cure. You should…."

The professor smiled and again shook his head.

"No, my dear. It's no use. The governments are not willing to listen to an old professor like me. No government or institute gave me the grant to research the communication channels used by viruses ten years ago when I was active in the field of research."

"But the world needs you now. No one probably knows as much as you do about these pathogens. We are all looking for a cure in the wrong direction. It is pointless how many viruses we kill. As long as we don't destroy their communication mechanism, they will always be a step ahead."

"That's correct. Now that you have figured out the right channel of defence, you can build a strategy to overcome the pandemic."

"Professor, I'll make a presentation to the board of directors of my company. I'll get their permission to invite you…"

"There is no need. When the pharma companies have bright researchers like you, the world has nothing to fear. Good night, Gayatri. It was nice talking to you."

The professor dismissed her as abruptly as he had begun the conversation. Gayatri had no option but to conclude the meeting. She thanked the professor again and left his home.

The phone had barely rung once but Sandhya jumped out of bed and accepted the call. The maternal instinct in her was stronger than the grip of sleep. She didn't want her daughter to wake up, especially since she had fallen asleep after great difficulty. Sandhya was herself dog tired from the office work during the day and wakeful nights caring for her daughter. She answered the phone in a sleepy voice.

Hello, who is this?"

"Sandhya, It's me! Gayatri from New York. I am sorry I woke you up. But I couldn't wait to share this news."

"What news" Sandhya's brain was still trying to figure out the context.

"The viruses do have a mind. You were right. I mean, not in the sense that you and I have a mind. But

they are communicating and developing strategies to defeat whatever we develop to kill them."

Sandhya was wide awake now.

"Why do you say so?" she asked.

"We carried out experiments in the lab. We found that they can communicate with each other even when they are in different hosts."

"How is that possible?"

"There's a lot of quantum physics involved. I will explain in detail later. But I just wanted to let you know that I am giving your name to the credit list of the paper we are presenting to the government. After all, you were the first person to declare that the virus seems to have a mind of its own!"

What followed next was going to be written in bold letters in the annals of history. NewMed Pharma presented a top-secret research paper to the Health Ministry, based on the findings of Gayatri's team and some recommendations. Within two days, Gayatri was invited by the Pentagon to give a presentation to senior officials. It took another week to convince the President of the necessity of accepting the recommendations. No one quite knew what pushed the final decision, but the shocking infection and death figures across the world seemed to have played a part.

Once the recommendations got the President's nod, the wheels of diplomacy began to churn as they had never before. Hotlines buzzed and e-mails on the secure networks flew by the hundreds every minute.

A week later, the highest authorities of their respective countries instructed all pharma companies of the world to halt whatever they were doing and begin the production of a particular drug – a secret cocktail of anti-viral medication. The factories producing these medicines were sealed and the consignments of the products were transported to government warehouses under the strictest security.

From there, packets of the medicine were loaded onto police vehicles that commenced their journeys to every town and village in every district of every country.

A week later, every doctor, every nurse, every paramedic, every schoolteacher and every government servant in every country of the world was contacted late Friday evening and ordered to report to their nearest police station at 8:00 AM the next morning. When they reached there, millions of these people across the globe heard a recorded message in their respective languages, which was identical in its content.

The message was simple – 'The governments of the world have united to bring an end to the coronavirus pandemic. The scientists of the world agree that there is only one way to defeat the virus. It can only be killed if every human being on this planet, irrespective of age, race, faith or colour, takes a particular medicine at the stroke of 9:00 AM today. You are an important link in this gigantic exercise.

Your job is to distribute this medicine to every individual in your locality and instruct them to swallow it at the stroke of 9:00.'

While the medicine was being distributed, every TV and radio channel and every social media platform began to play the message from the governments, urging people to eat the medicine at the stroke of 9:00.

The already exhausted world went into a panic. People ran out on the streets, they shouted; some protested. Others feared the worst. Some people threw away the medicines. But a majority of the world population swallowed the medicine within a two-hour window of time.

Twenty relatives accompanied Sandhya to the airport as she left for Amsterdam with her year-old daughter and husband. The post-COVID rush of people had not yet ebbed, but Sandhya and her husband had managed to secure flight tickets. They would reach Amsterdam just in time to attend the gala dinner on the eve of the Nobel Awards. Sandhya had not yet decided what she would wear for the actual award ceremony.

Gayatri and Sandhya were jointly awarded the Nobel Prize in medicine for finding the cure to the coronavirus. It was the first time that a non-medical person was being awarded this prize. But the jury was unanimous that Sandhya's insights had played a crucial role in changing the way scientists engaged in the fight against the pandemic.

After the masterstroke of making the entire population of the earth ingest the same medicine at the same time, the virus had drastically weakened. Gayatri and her team had found the chink in its armour by devising a method that would not allow the virus to communicate and develop a strategy to beat the new medicine. Although not everyone believed or followed the instructions to have the medicine, about 80% of the world population did. That was enough to disarm the deadly assassin. Health systems across the world were then able to manage the dwindling incidence of infection with routine medical care.

The plus point of the method was the unprecedented global cooperation between governments. It had taken a deadly disease that was seemingly threatening the very existence of humanity; but over the fortnight, most governments seemed to have matured to a new level of mutual understanding. It was only the beginning… but somewhere in the suburbs of New York, Professor Boyle believed that he was witnessing a new dawn of humanity.

NOSTOS

NOSTOS

-Debraj Moulick

Debraj Moulick is a Lecturer (English) at K.J. Somaiya Polytechnic, Mumbai, India. He is also a bilingual poet, short story writer and researcher in Science Fiction literature. Debraj also enjoys conducting workshops on creative writing and business communication. His writings have been published on various websites, magazines, and anthologies. Moulick did his M.Phil. in Indian Science Fiction from the Dept. of English, Mumbai University. He is a lifelong member of the Indian Association of Science Fiction Studies. Moulick has worked as an organising committee member as well as the Editor of an International Science Fiction conference in India. Debraj has provided expert lectures on various topics like Science Fiction and NEP, Thought Experimentation in Bangla Science Fiction, and the Importance of Translation in Science Fiction, among others. His research papers in Science Fiction have been published in peer-reviewed journals. His articles and official book reviews on Science Fiction have been published in Science India Magazine, Antonym, and Kalpabiswa.

I

The Cave

It had been almost, well I have lost count of the days, I have been in this cave on some remote island (that is my assumption). Well, not bad for a lazy ass like me, who hated his desk job and secretly hoped to get rid of all those codings, targets, style sheets, back bitching and so more.

Well, hope is a good thing according to the folks of Shawshank Prison, but it turned out to be dangerously pleasurable. Wait, it is time for my hot drink. You know, hobbits and I never miss a chance to gulp or drink. Let me have a sip and then I will start scribbling. Who is in a hurry to write? I don't have any deadline, oh good God. I don't need to catch any fast local. I don't have to half chew my crunchy wada to avoid the evening hour rush in JVLR. I have all the time, or I might be doomed here forever. Who cares? Let me have my drink.

II

The House

A few days ago, …

One sunny scorchy morning in the Bay. Time: 7:50 am

A single fellow is lying down on his king-size bed and occupying nearly most of it. One can see a tissue box, a spike booster, a laptop and a mobile phone. Oh, there are a few books like The Master and the Commander, The Lord of the Flies, The Tempest, Robinson Crusoe and

Tin Tin Comics among the books on the bookshelf beside the bed.

Ting tong.

One could hear the chuckles behind the door, where the maid's little daughter was extracting pleasure with every half-touched press upon the doorbell.

After the third bell, the creature moved a bit and uttered, "Aai Zawariya tham re" (just stop it, mother fucker) and shouted "Kal aajao (come tomorrow) and he dozed off to sleep, only to be forcefully up by 8:15 am.

With his bloodshot eyes and an inexplicable array of cuss words, he got down from his bed. The creature switched on his mobile and banged on the door of the washroom. The daily romance between him and his pot began. He started playing from his playlist which consisted of dystopian songs of Rafi, Mukesh and Kishore. He is one of the rarest animals who prefers sad and sombre songs in the morning. The green dot beside the name Pradip Patil blinked and it was on.

Pradip was having the best time of his day i.e., easing his bowel and browsing through Facebook, and Instagram and hobnobbing through the profile of Diya, a girl whom he secretly admires but too shy to admit even to himself and that too in front of no-one.

It was almost nine, which made Pradip gallop through the bathing zone and put up off his formals. He stuffed his giant mouth with vada pav. He was running towards the local station and somehow managed to position his body inside a relatively less stinky and minutely little less crowded boggy also known as a first-class in the locals of

Bay. They are characterized by red stripes i.e., pointing to the class distinction in public transport. Oh! God, Commies should have protested.

He boarded an auto afterwards.

III

The Office

Mumbai

Thamba. Kiiti ahay? (Stop it, how much?) He paid Rs 18 to the auto driver.

Good morning, Madam! Pradip greeted as he entered the cabin with a nameplate Mrs Asmita Ganguly, General Manager. The lady inside the cabin sported a polished look in a half-moon spectacle and a green embroidered saree. She looked up only to ignore him and shift her gaze towards her watch, "You are late again, I need the quarterly report before lunch, now buzz off." Pradip replied, "Madam, I got the data last night, I need at least two days to finish the report." (However, Pradip spoke all the words to himself only.)

In reality, he uttered a word, "Ok" and he left the cabin. Life is nothing sort of heaven when you have an affectionate and understanding boss like Mrs Ganguly, who would never guide you in work but would expect everything to be in order at her beck and call. Pradip smiled upon himself, he was slogging day and night, only to be mentally harassed at the workplace. However, the corporate slave returned to his work bay in the city of Bay which was stuffed with key chains and stickers from

Friends, Game of Thrones and some Tin Tin collectables. He started playing with Spiderman merchandise, he wondered if even Peter Parker had a loving boss like him.

He saw Mrs Ganguly leaving the cabin with a cellular phone in her hand and it struck him that lunch is knocking at the door, in short, his ass is on fire. With a half-fed soul and demotivated spirit, he indulged himself in the donkey work.

Oh! The curse of corporate life. The bane of Capitalism. Money is essential.

In between, he received a call from his Baba, "Start preparing for MBA, you slowpoke."

His education was forced. He wanted to be a sailor, but engineering cropped up. He had to take the job owing to parental pressure and the obligation of the great Indian society. His family and friends said he was a dull fellow without any kind of fire inside him. He is a mere ordinary fellow who won't ever shine in life. Thus, despite being a Pradip, he never glows. He is a laidback fellow without aims and ambitions.

Pradip finished his allotted work, not out of a sense of responsibility, but to avoid the loudmouth bitch, Asmita. He pressed the send option in the email. He hoped secretly (he knew, it was impossible) that he would get the appraisal. The office boy walked towards the heavily stressed man of the story and said, "Asmita Madam bula rahi hai." (Asmita Madam is calling you).

For the second time in the day, Pradip faced the angel in disguise Asmita and yes, it turned out to be nothing unusual, she was not at all satisfied and he received his token of love from her. Pradip's face glowed but with all the negative emotions like anger, disgust and irritation among others. He came out of the cabin. While everyone was having their snacks, he went to the washroom and banged the door. He sobbed and hit himself on his knee and it continued until it started to hurt. He washed his face and returned to his base. A voice asked, "Sir, coffee lau?" (Sir, shall I get a coffee?). It was the office boy, Rohit.

Pradip looked at Rohit and felt the pang of hunger, "Rohit get me some biscuits along with it." He switched off his system and went ahead to have a look at the outside world. It was already dark. Few of the office staff are engaging themselves with the option of working from home owing to some kind of panic about a tiny microbe. Still, two or three overburdened souls were gazing at their systems in the office. Cars were honking below and ants which were humans, in reality, were moving to and fro.

IV

The Bay

The corporate dog untied his lace unbuttoned the top button and started gazing towards the office ceiling. He sipped coffee occasionally between those vicious gazing episodes. He went down and visited the local supermarket to get some necessary stuff like milk powder, sugar, tea, and preserved meat among others. He took a train to Victoria Terminus and then a cab to Colaba market. He got a table at Baghdadi and gorged upon the fried chicken over there. He hardly gets any time on the weekdays and weekends are meant for sleeping, he missed the fried chicken. The waiter asked, "Aur Ek lau?" (One more?) Pradip said, "Bas re" (That is enough). He went ahead and had a few drinks of Old Monk at the andhera kayam rahein Gokul bar and it was almost 10:30. He went straight to the Gateway of India jetty. He paid some liquid cash and took a boat into the dark and deep Arabian Sea. The spirit of Captain Haddock was burning like a blue blistering barnacle, he dropped his mobile into the water.

While sailing away, he was constantly looking at his only companion. The friend who guides him home, when no one is with him. No one ever stayed with him, but her. Pradip was constantly smiling. He was breaking every shackle. He understood, that even his friend doesn't have her light, but it still survives. It still shines. He understood it is ok to be himself only. He understood it was okay to be the second fiddle. He understood it is okay, not to be a champion of life. It is ok to be weak and still make a presence. It is ok to be like his friend because it still glows. Pradip winked at his only companion, the glowing moon. He raised his hand to wave towards his beloved city and vanished into oblivion.

V

The Newspaper

Mumbai

IT Engineer from Prabhadevi is missing.

It is hereby reported that an IT Engineer named Pradip Patil working in an Indian Software Company at Prabhadevi has been missing since 10th March 2020. He was last seen leaving the office premises on the same date. Police have tracked his mobile near Gateway of India. It has been further reported that he took a boat and didn't return. A missing diary was lodged by the office boy of the same company at the local Police Chowky.

VI

Nostos

Sea

Food is running out. Pradip is growing restless. In the evening at around sunset, he goes out in search of food and comes back before it gets dark. He avoids going out in the daylight to avoid human contact. Pisces have reduced drastically, there are hardly any fish-eating birds around the island. Some boats often stop by the island to rest or just for the sake of the land. It was once in two to three days, but for one month, there has been not a single human being other than himself on the island. He hasn't seen any boats or other water transport in the Arabian Sea. He is getting restless not only because of food but also because he feels terrified. He wants to return to the Bay, to see if it is ok.

It took him almost a decade (one cannot count the time in this timeless place) to make a bamboo raft and his inexperienced hands made it worse. He could see the skyline of the bay. It is a busy route, the water route connects the city with places like Alibagh, Elephanta caves and other places in Konkan but Pradip hasn't seen a single moving boat or the steamer on the way since He noticed a mammoth sea vessel anchored at the middle, but not a single soul. This route is a paradise of seagulls. You must have offered them a morsel of pulse or a crumb of Pav while cruising over here. Well, you cannot spot any, not even one. The third-world Crusoe approached towards the Colaba jetty and noticed all the small boats and steamers being stranded and standing like a rock, yes, no waves too. The silence of the jetty was disturbing him, he was so much accustomed to the silence of the caves that he felt frustrated; he needed some crowd, some cheer, a group of people or at least a bark from a stray. The Gateway of India never appeared so unvoiced, so still, so lonely.

VII

Present Day

Colaba

Colaba is the star of the Bay, with places like the Taj Mahal Palace Hotel, Gateway of India, Office of the Commissioner of Police, it was always well maintained with neat roads, clean manholes and dustless sidewalks and so on. Pradip is shocked to see the garbage strewn all over the place. Effingut is locked, and the hairstyling salon is closed. He moves toward Regal Cinema; it looks like an old fort. Mondegar which used to bustle with energy is buzzing with silence. Colaba Market, the hub for street shopping is casting a serious look. The giant clock at the crossroads displays 13:00 hrs, 30th July 2020.

Pradip has never seen such empty streets, such empty sidewalks, such an empty Mumbai. He is hoping against hope, and he is proceeding towards Baghdadi. He wants to be in front of Gokul, located behind the Taj Mahal Palace Hotel. The roads are overflowing with plastic packets, carcasses, dirty papers etc. The place where he had his last civilized meal a few months ago, Bagdadi is covered with a holistic green cloth and Gokul displays a sign, closed until the end of the pandemic.

VII

No End

30th September 2020. Behind Taj

Pradip has been resting by the sidewalk, like a lost child. The phrase until the end of the pandemic is unbearable for him.

He has been roaming across Colaba, since the last ninety minutes and he hasn't come across a single human being. Leave aside the human beings, not a single animal too. There are no birds, the silence of his beloved city, the hellish view of the city without the soul, its people are tearing him apart. He wanted to run away from his claustrophobic professional life, so he went out for silence, but he loved this metropolis and now his beloved conurbation is a complete wasteland, this is horror. Pradip is feeling desiccated, is there a water tap? The eye of heaven shines in glory. Pradip tries to stand up but.......

............The pandemic is not yet over, no end.........

Note

1. Nostos is a Greek word that describes the theme of a journey by sea.

2. Shawshank Prison refers to the Prison mentioned in Stephen King's novella Rita Hayworth and Shawshank Redemption (1982).

3. JVLR is a busy highway in Mumbai.

4. Bay refers to Bombay (present-day Mumbai).

5. Crusoe is a homage to Daniel Defoe's central character in the novel Robinson Crusoe (1719).

6. Pav is a traditional Maharashtrian bread.

7. Wada is a traditional Maharashtrian dish.

SEEDS OF HOPE

SEEDS OF HOPE

-Varun Sayal

Varun Sayal writes high-voltage superhero action-adventure novels. If you like superhero stories with riveting action sequences, you will love the "Superheroes of the Multiverse" series.

Naresh stood on his eighth-floor balcony and gazed at the sun rising on the horizon as he sipped his morning coffee. Yellow beams of light emanated from behind a cluster of mud-coloured buildings a few kilometres away.

He then looked down and examined the small children's park just in the footsteps of their building. Like all the days in previous weeks, the rides were deserted, and the pavement was empty. A cursory look at the buildings nearby showed people standing on their balconies. Some were exercising, some just stared with weary eyes. But the ground was deserted. The eerie noise of wind blowing reminded Naresh of scenes created in post-apocalyptic movies.

He took a deep breath and turned around to see his six-year-old son standing right behind him, in an awkward pose.

"Bhow", little Pranav screamed. Naresh paused for a second and then did a mock action of getting afraid.

Pranav giggled and jumped into his arms. Naresh carefully kept his cup on a small table nearby as he caught the boy in his arms

"Paaapu, we are going to the park day after tomorrow, right?" There was a light of hope in the kid's eyes.

Naresh froze. Pranav has been planning to go to the park for around two weeks now, but with the recent lockdown extension, this was not going to be possible for another two weeks.

Naresh put the boy down and took a deep breath. "No beta. The government has announced an extension in a lockdown."

"Extension? Means what Paapu?"

"Means we can't go out except for getting essential supplies. The park will remain closed, and no one is allowed to even enter." He had made it a habit to not make any false promises to his boy and always speak the plain truth.

The smile on Pranav's face vanished and his little cheeks swelled with sadness as he watched his father go inside, "But you promised, Paapu!"

"I did and now I am telling you it's not going to happen. It's not in my hands." Naresh spread his arms on the side and sat down. He started scrolling through his smartphone.

"Daddaaa!", Pranav screamed and ran inside to his grandfather crying and complaining.

Naresh saw him dash to his grandfather's room, "Don't wake Daadu up..." but before he could complete his sentence the boy was inside the room sobbing and whispering to his grandfather.

Naresh went back to his screen. Stories of an increasing number of infections were coming from all major states in India. While some states declared themselves, free others were coming out as new hotspots. He put his smartphone aside, closed his eyes, and rubbed his face.

"Breakfast will be ready in a few minutes."

His wife's soft voice broke his concentration. He opened his eyes and smiled. Trushna stood with a small plate of fruits in her hand. "Where is our kiddo?"

"Here he is." Pranav's grandfather Dhyanchand came out of his room carrying him on his shoulder.

"Daadu, tell Paapu what you told me. We can go down." Naresh shot a glance at Dhyanchand.

Dhyanchand smiled. "I will just take him downstairs, till the lift and come back"

"Don't indulge him Bauji. We are in the red zone. The housing society is putting a thousand rupees fine on anyone who goes outside for no reason. Walking, strolling, and visiting the park are not allowed. I thought of taking him to the grocery shop, but with the crowd, I saw there last time, I don't want to take any risks."

Dhyanchand nodded. He looked at Pranav who was gazing at him eagerly as if waiting for a response. The old man put his hand on the kid's head. "No going out bete. Chalo, I will tell you a new story today."

"No … no … no..." Pranav shook vigorously and Dhyanchand had to let him down from his lap. "I want to go to the park. I want, I want, I want."

His constant badgering and high pitch of voice were now irritating Naresh.

"Ok first finish your fruits and then we will see." Trushna offered him a colourful plate of fruits.

She knew her son loved them.

"I don't want fruits; I don't want anything." Pranav slapped the plate, which fell to the ground crashing, with all the fruit pieces splattered on the floor.

"Pranav! Behave!" Naresh shouted at the top of his voice and stood up.

There was a momentary silence when everybody was still and then Pranav ran inside crying.

Trushna gave an angry glance to Naresh and then rushed after the kid.

Naresh sank back into his chair. This was not something he wanted to do but the reaction was a build-up of suppressed emotions within him. He missed taking Trushna and Pranav out for weekend lunches and dinners. He missed meeting his friends for drinks and missed the office parties. He missed his past life which now looked like a distant dream. This prolonged lockdown had taken its toll on everyone

Four hours later Naresh entered Pranav's room. The kid was playing a game on his mother's smartphone. As soon as he saw Naresh, he threw the phone on the bed, turned to the other side, and buried his head in the pillows.

Naresh smiled. "Buddy, won't you talk to your Paapu?" "No!" A loud voice.

"But I have a gift for you." Naresh's hands were behind his back. Pranav's eyes lit at the mention of a gift, but he still acted angrily.

"Ok, then if you don't want this gift, I'd give it to Dheeraj." Naresh did mock-acting of slowly receding out of the room.

"No! I want this gift." Pranav got up like a blitz and ran towards Naresh.

The father toyed for a few seconds with his son before giving him a small packet sealed in red cellophane.

Pranav quickly tore through the packet, opened it, and jumped with joy. There were several tiny seeds inside. Naresh had ordered these Masynth flower seeds online months back but they got delivered only recently. He had been keeping them secret from the child as a gift preserved for his birthday, but that day was not a bad occasion either.

Pranav kissed his father on the cheek and ran through the house yelling, with the seeds clasped tightly in his fist. He loved gardening and planting trees since he was a three-year-old and there couldn't have been a better present for him.

For the next hour and a half, the father-son duo spent planting the trees in a vacant pot kept on their balcony.

Dhyanchand peeped from the balcony door as he watched his son and grandson, engaged with dirty hands and sweaty brows. “This is summertime, and their growing season is receding. It won’t be easy for this plant to grow.”

Naresh turned back and smiled, while still pressing the freshly put mud on top of the seed. “Next seventy-two hours are crucial, Bauji. If it must grow, it will in this time, else there is no hope for it.”

Naresh looked at the glaring afternoon Sun and wiped the sweat off his forehead. “When will this grow up to be a big tree Paapu?”

“Well, that may take years, buddy.”

“When will I see golden-orange flowers in this plant?”

“Flowers take more time, but the first green leaves should come out within the next three days.”

The next three days were like a timer ticking for little Pranav. At first, he would go out on the balcony every fifteen minutes to check if the leaves had come out or not. Then every hour. Then before and after every meal. At times he would eat his whole meal sitting in front of the pot waiting for a tree to magically pop up. He had seen online the fast-forward time-loop videos of small roots and leaves coming out of a planted seed. He was expecting something similar. But that didn’t happen.

Three days passed. The afternoon came the evening and then the night. His cheeks puffed, his eyes watery, Pranav stood lachrymose in front of the empty pot.

Naresh came and stood behind him. "It's time for your dinner and then off you go to bed, mister."

"The plant didn't grow, Paapu."

"Yes, Daadu told you no. It's not the season. We will try with different seeds later." "Can we not dig it up and see what happened? It needs some help."

"No, beta." Naresh let out a sad chuckle.

Pranav turned back and walked to his room with heavy steps. He didn't even eat his dinner despite several attempts and slept hungry.

The next morning the kid woke up and dashed to the balcony right away. And a second later he woke up the whole house with his loud squalls. "Paapu, Daadu, Mumma, come here, come fast!"

Naresh and Trushna rushed worriedly. Dhyanchand also came, rubbing his sleepy eyes.

Pranav was excitedly pointing to the pot where they planted the seeds four days back. There was a small green shoot in the plant with a tiny green leaf.

Pranav got down on his knees and softly touched the petal. He turned back with tears in his eyes. "It grew, Paapu, it grew."

"Yes, kiddo." Naresh was overwhelmed with emotions. His throat was heavy. He walked and sat with his kid who was now smiling.

"What does this mean, Paapu? Why did it grow so late?"

"Well, it's the plant's way of showing us that despite all odds it persevered. Despite all hardships and adverse conditions, mankind too will bounce back. It means that there is hope for us after all."

SHORTCOMING

SHORTCOMING

-Nilesh Malvankar

Nilesh Malvankar's first Marathi Short Story collection "Hee Aagali Kahani" (Story with a difference) was published in 2016 under a scheme by Maharashtra Rajya Sahitya and Sanskruti Mandal. It won the Best Short Story Collection award by Padmagandha Pratishthan. He has published 99 Short Stories in 38 leading Marathi Diwali Magazines, Monthly Magazines and Newspapers. 10 of his Short Stories have won awards in Prestigious Short Story competitions. His Short Stories encompass a variety of genres like Science Fiction, Humour, Mystery, Fantasy, Horror and Romance. Nilesh also does Column writing "New Yorker" for a leading Marathi daily – Saamana. He also writes in a format popularly known in Marathi as 'ALAK' aka 'Ati Laghu Katha' (Tiny Stories). Many of his Tiny Stories have been featured in a popular radio show 'Alak chi Zalak' He lives in the USA with his wife and 2 kids. He has over 20 years of Experience in the field of Information Technology.

A large crowd had gathered at the press conference hosted by renowned researcher Allen Mhaske. Despite the crowd, everyone was maintaining social distance. All the prominent journalists from major newspapers, TV channels, and news portals were present at the conference wearing masks and rubbing sanitisers on their hands.

Everyone was eagerly waiting for Allen. Allen Mhaske was not only a researcher but also a billionaire. He had made all this fortune from his research. He had the honour of making the world's first automatic car. Allen was one of the most intelligent people in the world.

COVID-19, which is known all over the world, was thought to be caused by bats. Allen was involved in research related to bats for many years. His favourite subject was bats and their immunity towards the coronavirus.

Allen Mhaske's secret experiments on COVID-19 were being conducted at his laboratory. The experiments were rumoured to be at an advanced stage. People generally have a notion that scientists are crazy people. Moreover, Allen was a billionaire. So, he was assumed to be doubly crazy. It was also rumoured that he was conducting the trials of the drug he was making for COVID-19 on himself.

Everyone had gathered at the conference hoping that many such questions would be answered at today's press conference. The breakthrough was going to prove a world changer. Success meant deals of multi-million dollars with Big pharmaceutical giants in the offing.

Suddenly there was some murmur. Everyone looked in the direction of the voice. Allen was coming towards the stage. After reaching the stage, he looked at the crowd and said, "I'm sorry, guys."

Everyone was flummoxed.

"My friends, the reason I called this conference today was because I was convinced that I had found a solution to eradicate COVID-19, but..."

His long pause started to make people nervous. People were getting desperate with every passing day. They had high hopes for Allen.

"But I noticed that there are a few big glitches in that solution. So, some more tests need to be done. And if those problems go away, I will come to meet you all again. I was planning to cancel this conference. But let me reiterate that despite some difficulties, research is moving in the right direction. I hope that within the next few months, I will be able to give you good news by overcoming the difficulties that are currently prevalent."

"But what exactly are these problems?"

"Does it cure COVID even though there are glitches?"

"If it can cure one of the COVID, why make a fuss about a few side effects? Anyways, all the drugs have some or the other side effects."

"Is it true that you are testing this drug on yourself?" Journalists threw all sorts of questions at Allen.

"Sorry guys. I would have loved to answer all of these questions. But at this stage, even I don't know the answers to some of these questions myself. Moreover, there are contract obligations due to which I cannot reveal right now. I have to maintain some secrecy. I'm really sorry. "

Allen ended the conference by answering some of the innocuous questions from reporters.

Mostly disappointed, everyone started to disperse. Few reporters were interested in personal interviews or at least a bite. But Allen politely refused all the requests saying that he was not feeling well and needed some privacy.

Allen was not unwell, but he realised that his hands were shaking slightly towards the end of the conference. Normally, he would have driven directly to his laboratory. But today he was getting tempted to take a stroll in the small forest nearby. Since his hands were still trembling a bit, Allen switched to fully automatic mode and drove off in his fully automatic car toward his lab. He entered his laboratory immersed in deep thought. His research on COVID-19 drug was almost successful. He intended to announce it today. It was true that he was testing the drug on himself. The drug was showing miraculous results. However, in the last few days, he was beginning to feel the side effects of that treatment. Initially, those were mild. But day by day its intensity was increasing. Allen's habits were beginning to change. At first, he controlled it. But lately, the situation was out of his control. The same thing was happening now. He was trying hard to control his mind. But in the end, he gave in to the habit caused by the side effects of the drug. Allen had a full-fledged gym in his lab. He had erected a beam a few days ago in this gym as a result of the strange habit he had succumbed to. He went below the beam. He caught the beam with both his hands. Then he lifted his body and placed his feet over the beam bent at knees and the next moment he started hanging upside down like a bat.

THE DEAL

THE DEAL

-Pragya Gautam

(Translated from Hindi by Kshama Gautam)

Pragya Gautam is a Lecturer in the subject of Biology. She has been writing children's stories, poems, articles and science stories in reputed science magazines continuously for the last 9 years. Along with teaching, she is active in environmental protection and Science talks broadcast on All India Radio. She has written science plays for Corona awareness. Some of her known works are Alaukik aur anya kahaniyan (Science fiction collection), Translation of many science fiction stories into regional languages and English. Some of her accolades are as follows: * District Level Best Teacher Award (2006). Kavya Vibhuti (2017), * Vigyan Sahitya Ratna (All India Poetry, * Story and Arts Council (2018), * C.V. Raman Science Award (2019), * Honoured for best work in the tribal area (2019), * Kavitai World Science Competition 2020 (Third Prize), * National Science Communicator Award (2021) by National Media Foundation, New Delhi, * Sahitya Mandal (Nathdwara) Hindi Sahitya Bhushan Award (2021), * Award by Science Council Prayag.

An inward village of Africa

There was an ultra-modern house in the lap of nature, away from the rush and ruction of the city. The lawn of Mr Morris's cottage was shining with the soothing sun of dusk. Morris was throwing a keen look at his garden sitting in a chair. Mary (Doll 7) could grasp all that was running in his head. She was engrossed in watering the plants and tidying up the flower beds from the yellow fallen leaves at the same time. He adjusted his hat a little and stretched out his legs on the chair and yawned. Today he slept whole the day long so felt lazy. His brain demanded snacks and coffee. Annie (Doll 6), began to move her hands, working in the kitchen. She came out with an exquisite antique tray that contained a cup of coffee and vegetable rolls.

"Thanks, Annie, so kind of you dear!" He threw an appealing smile holding a mug from Annie's hands.

"It was the least I could do for you, Morris." She returned the smile.

Morris looked at the drowning sun while sipping the coffee. The green and velvet-like hill appeared like a dark monster when the last rays of the sun which crowned the hill, got lost. The tints of red and yellow also mingled in the lake before him and the water became inky. Morris loved this sight as the dark nature seemed concentrated. There remained no difference in its objects. The lights of his garden turned on.

People here believe that Morris is the owner of the unfathomable property. And on that account, he was able to build a paradise even in this backward village. Having completed a century of his age, Morris had gifted this smart cottage to himself lately on his hundredth birthday and celebrated the day here only. This prosperous man had become the object of curiosity for the villagers of the surrounding areas. But he hardly moved out. Here in desolation, these seven Robo Dolls were with him and being his companions, looking after him without any complaints and botheration. He was spending his life delightedly with extreme tranquillity and constant flow.

"Stop Mary, garden time is over." The instruction came in his brain and instantly water sprinkles stopped and Mary kept down the instruments. She entered the house thanking Morris. It was 7c'clock. The chair reminded him in a mechanical but very sweet voice that his friend Harry was waiting for him in a virtual drawing room. Morris instructed it to go inside and the chair, crossing the grass over the lawn, walking onto the cemented paths constructed in between flowerbeds reached the main way to the front door which was decorated with brown tiles. As soon as he reached there the front door opened automatically with the sound, "Welcome Morris." Let it be so many times, this door never forgot to welcome him each time. He thanked the door for its etiquettes and humbleness.

Morris got inside rising from the chair. Nurse Rosy (Doll 5) was there to assist him. He reached his bedroom with the help of Rosy. He changed his clothes and freshened up in the washroom. Now he came into the relaxing and half-lying position. He turned on his computer and opened the virtual drawing room. This was his daily routine. Harry was sitting a little anxious on the couch in the drawing room.

"Harry, you're looking tensed. What's the matter?"

"Tremendous fuss is going on Morris....there is a global crisis before us," Harry mumbled softly.

"Calm down Harry...what has happened like that? Above all, what do we old people do with this global crisis?" Morris replied nonchalantly. But Harry did not affect his behaviour and continued speaking.

"The future of the human race is in peril. We won't exist...no one would exist...not even you...."

"I have already lived more than enough; I have no fear of any kind. Moreover, we elderly people don't have any solution regarding this worldwide hazard. shall we start playing Rummy?" Morris displayed a cold reaction as he was no more curious to know about this.

Harry felt irritated. He had come to Morris to talk a lot about this topic. He did not expect this kind of response from this wealthy and intellectual old man. He had a great network of contacts with influential people around the world....and besides, he was always ready with a solution for any problem. He did not know Morris for a long time. They just casually met twice or thrice and became friends. Morris hardly walked out but they met online daily.

He started playing unwillingly. He took his leave after losing the game twice. "Poor old buddy..." Morris turned off the computer spreading his lips.

He had porridge for dinner and surrendered himself to the soft bed. It was 9 o'clock at night. His house became auto-locked from the inside. His acquaintances knew that he did not prefer to meet anyone after 9 pm.

Sitting beside him, witty (Doll4) got activated. Her eyes shone in the dim light of the room.

"Latest news updates witty...?"

"Planning of VH Lee, mission-7 has been disclosed."

"I know that. Anything new? He asked picking a bowl of black grapes from the side table.

"There have been many months since Lee has returned from Planet X. thenceforth, he attended meetings and participated in political affairs. But at present, he has disappeared from China...he is hidden somewhere...after the disclosure of mission -7, the pursuit for him has been prompted."

"Now let him be anywhere, he has definitely known about this disclosure. He is indeed a vicious man...why does he hate human beings this much? He is, after all, a human being.... say little defective..." He smiled out of sarcasm.

"Then, Morris let me tell you a story about why he hates human beings this much..."

Witty (Doll-4), now started the tale. The remaining three Dolls of the bedroom had also been activated.

VH Lee

Lee was born around fifty years before from now in China. Chin cong and Zeng Hui spent nine months in preparations to welcome their newborn baby. She was always in touch with her doctor and everything was fine. But when the baby was born, it was shocking for the couple. The baby looked normal nevertheless the skin of his legs and hands was scaly and weird. There were light red patches also present on the skin. His face also was not beautiful...it was longer than usual and the head was big and bald. When a few tests regarding the infant's health were held, there was no particular disease found. The development of the body and brain was also normal. The doctor told that if it was a normal allergy those spots would disappear after a certain period but if these spots were due to mutation, they would be present forever. As the mental, as well as physical health of the baby, was excellent there was nothing to be worried about.

Cong and Hui were despondent. But nothing could be done now. As a matter of fact, the skin of an embryo is created after four to five months...and that time also if she had come to know of that. what could have been done? She could never go for an abortion.

The baby had been named Cong Lee. He began to grow up. As he grew up the skin of his legs and hands became wrinkled. The spots on his skin grew more and more and turned darker. By God's grace, his face did not contain those marks.

Lee was admitted to the school but children used to make fun of him. He was so intelligent that it was difficult for teachers to teach him. Some frustrated teachers, as well as students, would torture him. A few children and teachers who were at his side had to be quiet as they were all together most of the time. He would feel extremely insulted and disregarded. After getting primary education Lee quit school and joined a virtual classroom. He would stay at home and whenever he went out, he would cover his head, legs and hands. He carried on his studies at home. He had no friends. After a few years, he had a sister. This time his mother got the DNA of the embryo tested at the initial stage. His sister was normal. Now he felt more neglected.

Lee grew up and got a Master's degree. He had done a lot of skill development courses while staying at home. But how long he would remain at home...he had to look for a job...then had to marry... he used to ponder over these things, would dream and then he heeded on his face and body. Then he would lose all excitement. He hated himself...he tried to commit suicide so many times. His parents would inculcate him and motivate him to go out.

Eventually, Lee stepped out of the house but with zero confidence. He did not look for a job and set out for an uncertain journey. During this journey, he met Buddhist monks and began to be with them. They accepted him heartily. He wandered about with monks for many years. After stepping out of the house he came across the reality that there were so many other people also in this world who were neglected like him. Post several days, the number of mutant infants increased. Then research was done on the genome of these infants. Consequently, the secret behind this unfolded and the truth came out that the DNA of some kind of virus had linked with these infants' DNA. Many years ago, spread a pandemic which was a viral disease that originated in Wuhan city of China. Millions of people died because of this epidemic. The people who were saved had been resistant to this disease. Some of these people contained this virus in their blood in the inactive form... the virus came to the embryo from the mother's body.. the genome of the embryo is connected with viral DNA inside the cell. Viral DNA was present in his body and inside his every cell.

Out of contempt people used to call these infected people like him, 'viro human.'

Witty paused for some time. Morris's face turned garbled hearing the word 'Viro human.' Morris was acquainted with the story of Lee yet he perceived Lee's pain whenever he heard his story by Witty.

"Go ahead, Witty," he observed.

"One day Lee happened to meet a man like him and he started working with him. Besides, he would keep in contact with the same kind of people through the internet and he formed a secret organization. To the people of this organization, he would give provoking speeches. He used to tell them that this disease was a boon for them as they were stronger and more intelligent than human beings. He gained expertise in preaching in the company of Buddhist monks. He continued running his business with his wit and apart from that, he got himself involved in preaching and social services. He had a victory over his contempt through his temperament. He was getting popular....and it was the right time to enter politics.

Being active in politics for many years he succeeded in reserving a place in the parliament of China. He got the chief position for the huge Space project 'Planet X' remaining in parliament. Now people would call him VH (Viro Human) Lee, out of love not of aversion.

"Afterwards, what events took place, you must have an idea, Morris..." Witty stopped for a while.

"Don't you want to know about Planet X Morris? Honey (Doll-3) responded in no time. Honey kept updates on Planet X every moment through her sensors. She had records of its every plan regarding past, future and present.

"Honey, I know about the pre-set form of Planet X, but I don't have any advanced knowledge about its history and objectives."

"Ok, Morris then no other romantic story...I will explain to you about this today.... here I go"-

Planet X

Planet X took its form under an enterprising project. It was a humongous space station in which there were numerous closed structures. An artificial environment was created in this station. Its construction was initiated thirty years ago from today. Its foundation was underlain by the great scientist Wang Chin of China. The time had come when human beings built permanent abodes outside the boundaries of the earth. Its theoretical model was ready, to which a real form had to be given by processing several steps.

It had been situated near Mars. Initially, resources had been arranged from the earth...then this colony had been made independent. This colony was being designed by the Quantum computer 'Extreme 2050Q.' There was an unfathomable store of nuclear and solar energy...and there were mineral reserves, stretched over millions of kilometres in the form of the asteroid belt. E2050Q was engrossed in designing unique nano-objects to build residential structures in space. Apart from that, it had designed a lot of bacteria that produced oxygen, receiving nutrients from space matters. Also, it designed lower-class plants.

This incident would be of about post five years when in a session of parliament, there was to be elected a political delegation to control the activities related to the construction of Planet X. Lee unanimously got a membership in this assembly. Soon he got a golden opportunity to visit Planet X.

That tiny colony was a wonderful and winsome world. This extremely systematic and well-arranged colony contained many closed domes that were connected. There had been built a township out of lightweight materials in a huge dome which was full of a lot of skyscrapers. An artificial environment, as well as gravity, was created inside this. A plant was settled for the creation and renewal of environmental gases. The other dome which was attached to this dome contained thermal and nuclear power plants to supply energy. In a dome, there had been established in many industries. Mining work of matters was also under process. Finally, Lee was brought to visit laboratories where computers were busy designing unique matters and creatures. Analysis of the pieces of asteroids and comets were being executed.

Lee felt like he was in dreamland. And that very moment while wandering in this dreamland he dreamt with open eyes to settle down here for lifelong and all other people would also be like him, who would be called Viro Humans. No man had to be normal...his ambition began to release through his every nerve.... only we must live here...only us...all contempt, struggle and all human beings would be left on earth.

A cheerful youth named Ted Zao was assisting Lee to visit the laboratory.

"Have a look sir, these bacteria have been designed by us. They turn poisonous metals into useful salts, out of which many other worthwhile things can be created. They are autotrophic and we have increased their production capability many times by using gene technology. We have developed new aquatic and terrestrial ecosystems here according to the atmosphere. Have a look here...."

Numerous types of various creatures, swimming in the huge tank were displayed there.... tiny grasslands and on it, there were hopping insects and creeping worms...

"It's a unique world, Ted. I am convinced of your tedious work. Haven't you started experimenting on big creatures as well as human beings?

"This is only the remaining part. Experiments are going on. Such genes which could increase their immunity, as well as radiation-bearing capability to several times larger, would be inserted into the large creatures. Afterwards, colonization would be started."

"Ted, what do you think about me? The virus genome is associated with our genome...our immunity is greater than you human beings."

"Sir, why should you take this risk? Some other Viro Human would be called here for the experiment."

Lee had returned to the earth and at the same time, was becoming stronger day by day the daydream, which took birth in his brain. In the next meeting of the parliament, he proposed that as a team of workers, Viro Humans had to be sent there since their adaptation capacity and immunity are much better than human beings. His proposal had been accepted. Initially, a team of fifty people was sent there. Now Viro Humans were working in plants and industries. They were assisting the scientists in laboratories. And truly they proved that they could work more efficiently than human beings.

"And then what happened...you already know Morris," Honey said completing her story.

"Both of you did not mention Mission 7 in your stories." Morris observed putting a grape into his mouth."

"Our Storytime is over... Mission 7 would be proceeded by

Pretty (Doll 2)."

"Dear Morris, Mission 7 was a giant conspiracy which was weaved by Lee and soon he was about to execute that.... listen further..."

Mission 7

"Lee was constantly in contact with his companions at Planet X. He would say, "Friends, the eight per cent of DNA in humans is virally originated but in our case, ten per cent of our DNA is made up of the DNA of the virus. Hitherto such mutations negatively on the capacity of the brain yet this is a matter of great pleasure now as these mutations are positive and ascending. We are more capable and more developed humans. We know the fact that the environment on Earth is continuously changing, and Space is under arduous conditions. Man is a feeble creature...and this breed must be taken to an end now. Only our breed will survive on Earth as well as in Space. Men call us ugly...in upcoming years; measurement of beauty would also be changed."

In the upcoming years, many teams of Viro humans were sent to Planet X. They were called workers but they had influence everywhere. A lot of secret experiments were taking place under their supervision. The great reason behind this was their strong immunity system. At the last stage, a vaccine was being developed for seven intensely hazardous viral and bacterial diseases. In a microgravity environment vicious kind of mutations takes place. Subsequently, a vaccine that is prepared in this kind of environment is more effective. Viro Humans were employed as lab technicians. The work was in rapid progress. The trial of the vaccine of phase 1 was successful. The team of scientists was delighted with the rays of sunshine.

When nugatory virus samples were being destroyed, Dr Chih Ming who was working there realized that a few Vials were less in number...it was confirmed after rechecking the data. But who did this? The task was so carefully implemented that there was no clue found. Lab technicians were under suspicion. The whole staff of the lab was changed. Travelling between Earth and Planet X was seized. Investigation for the lost vials was started but they were not found. Just after returning to earth, Lee participated in a meeting. In later meetings, he sent information about his falling sick.

Investigation agencies had started a search. But Lee is extremely cunning. No one could find him. If Lee has those samples then there might be a catastrophe on earth." Pretty ended her story.

"That's why I say that this is the time for clever and wise people like Lee. We, humans, are now outdated..." Morris said grabbing the last remaining grapes together in his mouth. "The grapes of Harry's orchard are delicious." He added.

"You never feel scared, Morris?" Pretty asked surprisingly.

"What kind of fear should be there for an old man like me? Fenny (Doll1), do you have any idea what would happen next? Would Lee be ever caught?

"Of course! Morris, don't forget it is said that 'the problem with the world is that the intelligent people are full of doubt while the stupid people are full of confidence.' The investigation agencies of China are in search of Lee. Recently according to current news, a news channel in China has postulated that they have found the whereabouts of Lee. He may any time be arrested."

"That's correct! Stupid people are full of confidence. My dear dolls, the intellectual experience of an old man like me, says that it is not a kid's stuff. The media of China is misleading people. And. what wrong has he done? Years ago, these people only invented a virus that happened to destroy the whole of the world. Lee is a product of that destruction. This inhumanity is in his genes moreover he is gifted with hatred. He has this virus in his blood as well as in his cells and besides, it is in his thought process.

These people are only responsible for the birth of millions of companions Lee, scattered in this whole world. The subjugation of one Lee would create thousands of other Lees. But who is this Lee to destroy humanity? Nature shall do its task itself. You see, Planet X would be taken over by Viro Humans. Lee would have a deal to save human beings who live there. He would want to be a president in the bargain."

"You're indeed a very wise man, Morris. A very good night to you and have sweet dreams." All four dolls spoke in chorus.

There ran a soft laugh on Morris's lips. "Good night dolls, thanks for talking." He turned off the main switch of the system. All dolls turned inactive. All objects at home now were normal objects. He proceeded towards the washroom lazily. He glanced at himself in a human-sized mirror in the washroom. A face full of wrinkles...hat which was hanging over the eyes... thick spectacles...oversized hanging shirt.

"Old Morris! You have to scare...humanity is in peril... Hahahaha...great! Hahaha..." He burst into laughter.

"Lee would never be caught...China is making a fool of people" He was mumbling. He removed his hat and hung it then he took away the mask from his face softly... He removed his clothes....in front of the mirror stood a six-foot tall, robust man of tightened body, fully covered with spots in place of a wrinkled face and sagging skin. An ugly longish face whose lips twitched because of an ironical smile....in his eyes there were floating many illegible secrets.

THE EARTHS OF
OUR PAST

THE EARTHS OF OUR PAST

-Charu Thapliyal

Charu divides her time between her Doctoral Research at the Department of Philosophy, Delhi University and as the co-founder and Chief Editor at MB Publishing House, India's first self-publishing platform dedicated to spreading holistic living. Her areas of interest include Indian Philosophy, Metaphysics, Consciousness Studies, Indian Psychology and Sanskrit Text Studies. She is a certified Philosophical Counsellor as recognized by the American Philosophical Practitioners Association and a recipient of the Indian Philosophical Congress Medal (2011-14). She regularly writes on various topics of interest to civil society for popular magazines. Through her venture MB Publishing House, she seeks to one day take forward her motto of Swadhyaya or "Self-improvement and cultivation of the spirit through reading books" to every house in the world. Her parent group Mad Buddhas is involved with spreading holistic living in creative ways through animations, graphic design, illustrations, organising national spiritual events, seminars and meets on topics of research in spiritual science etc.

WELCOME TO THE 275th OFFICIAL 4D-EARTH TOUR. KINDLY FASTEN YOUR SEATBELTS. PLEASE TAKE YOUR WELCOME KIT FROM THE FRONT OF THE BUS. OUR TOUR WILL COMMENCE SHORTLY.

The loudspeaker at the end of the bus played a light classical track as Ralphio groaned. He was already in his seat with his seatbelt fastened and had heard this message replay in his headphones for a good fifteen minutes! He was never going to go for any tour on the recommendation of his wife again. Much good it did him listening to her, he thought as he humphed into his coffee. His eyes followed a tall pimply gentleman with dishevelled brown hair who had just got onto the bus wearing a blue uniform coat with a matching hat. He looked like the tour guide.

Finally, some information!

"Welcome to the official 4D Earth Tour Bus. My name is Shin Stamprickle. I'll be your guide for today" the pimply man said pointing to his name tag.

"Please hold onto something. This is going to be a bumpy ride. In another ten minutes, we are going to start the tour as we hurtle thousands of light-years into space to travel to the other end of our galaxy to see ancient 4D Earth in person. This tour has been subsidised by the Ministry of Humanistic Concerns, please line up your tickets so I can give you the discount coupons which can be redeemed at our gift shop later" he spoke in a rehearsed voice as he moved along the rows of the bus and people started shuffling their bags to find their tickets.

"High schoolers taking this trip for their galactic history class credit please open your welcome folder within which you will find attached the official journal entry as received from Mother Gaia on the day the split happened. This should contain all the information needed for your annual report and…."

"Excuse me, sir. What do you mean by 'split'?" a blonde girl with pigtails who seemed to be about ten years of age asked. Shin smirked. The young ones never knew until you told them. He loved seeing the look on their little faces as he did. The poor girl was probably on this bus with her parents and had been told to sit quietly in her seat without the context of where she was going or why. Shin detested such parents.

"I'll tell you, missy, we are……." He stopped to look at the light above his head flicker ever so slightly.

Suddenly a thundering sound resounded in the air as if a whip had struck the top of the bus. A child screamed as another one started to cry.

"CLOSE YOUR EYES, EVERYONE! IT IS TIME" Shin bellowed as all trace of light vanished from the bus and the children on board started crying anticipating in their energy bodies something was going to happen. He held on tight to the pole in front of his seat. He had flown off the bus once only to integrate in the middle of nowhere. Not this time, no sir. He was going to hold on for dear life.

A crackle of electricity arose from within the roaring engines of the bus and before Ralphio knew it he was gone!…

And before he could think about where he had gone, he was back. The entire bus shuddered and shook, "Damn these new tour agencies, smooth operation my foot!" thought Ralphio as the lights turned back on. His grandfather was from the earth, or so his grandmother had told him, were it not for him he would never have come on this bus.

The passengers gaped in true amazement as each panel of the bus rolled down revealing large transparent glass panes surrounding them, rendering the bus a see-through aura that gave them a 360-degree view of space. Ralphio saw his dangling legs. It seemed like he was suspended mid-air. For someone looking at them from afar, it would have seemed that 40-odd people were floating mid-air, sitting on invisible chairs, an invisible force field somehow keeping them all oriented in the same direction.

"Look, papa! It's the Earths!" the girl with the pigtails shouted pointing to their right.

Ralphio turned to look in the direction and sure enough, he saw them there. Some hundred kilometres away from the bus were the two Earths, both identical but one greener in its brown hue and a cleaner blue in its blues than the other one.

"Ladies and Gentlemen" Shin cleared his throat as he pointed to the Earths with both his hands, "Presenting to you the 4D and the 5D twin Earths spinning seamlessly one next to the other.

Children will see them as they are, adults with spiritual vision blockage due to old age might need to use the special dimensional shift glasses in your welcome kit.

Look closely my little ones. This is a lesson in cosmic history which was one for the ages." He looked out the window. He had been on these tours ever since they started but this was the moment which still took his breath away every single time.

Ralphio followed Shin's hands and looked on in awe as he saw two seemingly identical Earths spinning next to each other, massive balls of dust and water hanging in the void.

He closed his eyes, crossed his feet, clasped his hands and became one with his breath. He entered into a meditative state to see what was not visible to his eyes. The second Earth was the 5D-Earth, much lighter in vibration than the 4-D Earth, obviously, but this lightness of vibration came not from the Earth herself but from the people on it, he noticed. He felt like he was looking at the origin of life itself and a deep wave of gratitude overcame him as he opened his eyes and looked at the Earth. He felt like he could sit and look at the Earths in silence for all eternity.

"Hello, excuse me, hello, am I audible?" Shin's voice echoed around the bus as if coming from all around them as he tapped on his microphone. Ralphio groaned again.

"Many many moons ago circa 2020, there was present the 4D Earth as the cosmos knew it back then. Apart from the three spatial dimensions, in the 21st century, humans had started to explore the fourth dimension which gave them access to a unified perception of the Self-cutting across time and they realised that they could travel in time by being in high meditative states. However, not everyone had access to these abilities. They were reserved for the serious seekers and students of consciousness. As the time for the next jump approached it was noted that humanity had pushed the consciousness of the planet's energy body, Mother Gaia to the extent that she had to unleash an unexpected plague upon herself to rid herself of the karma of the humans who were not ready for the jump."

"Err…when you say, jump sir, what exactly do you mean?" a little boy with blue eyes and copper hair sitting in the third row from the front asked.

"The jump in the consciousness, of course, laddy!" Shin jumped from his seat and twirled to face the audience, a twinkle in his eye. This was his favourite part. "Exactly like a photon jumps from one frequency band to another!"

"Earth was shifting into 5D you see. Those who were not ready for the jump were going to vacate their bodies as per their soul contract with Mother Gaia while those who did not wish to leave their bodies but were not mentally prepared for the leap were going to stay back on split Earth which was going to vibrate in the 4th dimension. Yes, this was the infamous COVID-19 that swept Earth by storm in the year 2020 my friends! It is one of the perfect examples of disaster management responses our galaxy has seen in many light years! It was quite ingenious on the part of Mother Gaia truly!"

Shin waited till the moment of silence opened, he practically knew what response to expect from his audience now.

"High schoolers, you may now open the journal entry by Mother Gaia herself on her tipping point day, tucked inside your welcome kit and see what I mean straight from the horse's mouth." Pages ruffled as everyone switched to their reading glasses and immersed themselves in the story of Gaia. Shin sat down and shut his eyes, perfect time for a good snooze while everyone read. This would make an exact 20 minutes according to his schedule.

Ralphio opened his welcome kit and took out the paper which had been scanned from a diary, xeroxed and shared with everyone. He started to read.

"It was a beautiful day and I sat in the garden with the sun shining gently on me. A soft breeze caressed my cheek as if telling me that the wait for my son was not mine alone. I stood up and readied myself. The place had to be tidied up, there was a lot of work to be done. I filled a basket with fresh fruits for him. I knew his favourite were mangoes and I put a lot of those aside for him. I went to the garden front and watered the flower bed. Rows upon rows of roses had been planted for him. Nothing but the sweetest-smelling flowers should greet my son when he comes back. I went to the stream flowing behind our house and filled a jug with cold, clear water for him to quench his thirst when he came back tired from work. He worked hard all day long and the least I could do was show him all the love I have for him. Lately, he had been stressing out a lot. Maybe there was some problem at work, I thought.

Suddenly I heard footsteps and snapped out of my reverie. My heartbeat escalated. My son was back! Oh, how could I possibly explain my joy in mere words!

I ran up to the front gate and stood on my toes to get a better look at my boy. He stood there all dark and brooding. He seemed angry at something, someone. I saw him standing near the roses I had just watered. He glanced at them, plucked them and threw them aside in a heap. He shouted at me for wasting precious space and crashed into the basket of fruits I had just put down. He tipped it over with all his might and shouted some more. I just stood there and patiently waited for him to see me and calm down but before that could happen, he saw the jug of water I had just brought for him. He shouted some more foul words, spit into the water and spilt it on the grass saying that it was not clean enough to be consumed now and started cursing me for not paying attention to his needs. He saw me standing at the entrance of our house, smiling, waiting patiently. He came over and whacked me square on my face. He pulled my hair, kicked me twice, complained about my wasteful efforts and reprimanded me for being such a lousy mother. I smiled all the while and took one last loving look at his face before he left for the day.

I got up, went and sat by the stream and started to clean myself.

My darling son would be back tomorrow and as Mother Gaia, I had to make sure to satisfy all his needs when he came back. I do suffer when he unleashes his wrath on me, his masculine energies on the rise for the last thousand years, without sufficient balancing divine feminine in his aura yet. But I smile and wait for the day when he will finally realize how loving, caring and forgiving I am. Until that day my routine follows. So, I get up from the riverbank, smile and go back to the house to wait for my son to come back for now.

Love him as much as I do, I have to shift my consciousness soon and I hope he will come along on the journey or else like many of my children species before him I will have to leave him behind. I close my eyes and pray for his return to me."

Ralphio looked up from the paper as tears started to dwell in his eyes, the vibration of these words echoing in his soul as he heard Shin's voice coming from behind him bringing him back to the invisible bus.

"You see ma'am, no one knows exactly when the shift happened but with each day that the virus spread on Earth the planet became lighter and moved higher." Ralphio heard Shin tell a passenger.

"Many people turned inward when they were locked at home to contain the spread of the virus and their quest to realize their errors put them in a higher vibration. They could move onto the new Earth with the realization that they are not just the body but they are souls. As they understood deeper aspects of the law of karma and reincarnation it became clear to them why COVID-19 was supposed to happen the way it did. It was divine intervention, purely. Those who aligned themselves with this new plan of the planet survived and moved onto 5D which gave them access to a 'unified timeless perception of the Self along with the consciousness of the Soul-Self' however, many people failed and they had to stay back in 4D."

"Those who could stay in harmony with their fellow man and with nature were bumped up to 5D. They were the ones who started respecting nature again. Taking only as much as they needed, they turned vegetarian, realizing that animals are not food but complex sentient beings present on earth to experience Gaia consciousness just like the souls in the human bodies. It was a tough decision for Mother Gaia as she loved all her children equally but some souls had their karma bank full. There was nowhere to go but empty it all."

Ralphio took off his glasses and looked out the window gloomily at the blurry Earths in front of his eyes. When his grandmother left her human body in 2020 her soul had travelled across space and taken birth on the planet Pandoria where their family then had sprawled. She had retained all her earthly memories on account of her karma and knew her husband was still alive as a human but she could not tell which dimension Earth he was on. It took a long sip of water for Ralphio to clear his head as he wondered which of the twin Earths in front of him his grandfather was on. The lush green blue 5D Earth or the brown blue 4D Earth.

Ralphio thought back to memories of his grandfather passed to him in thought by his grandmother. He was a fairly kind man with gentle words flowing from his mouth, he did well to all and did not ever cheat or lie to anyone, his grandmother had told him, but he was a voracious meat eater and that was one habit that he had not been able to give up. Now the question was, was that one habit strong enough to make him stay back on 4D or not, Ralphio thought as he peered from the glass windows at the edge of 4D Earth as the bus made a slow revolution of the twin earths.

Ralphio closed his eyes again and asked Mother Gaia to guide him. There was a whisper in his ear -

"Killing animals for food is the highest akarma a soul can accrue on earth."

He jolted his eyes open with a start as tears started gushing down his eyes. He could suddenly feel the pain of all the souls whose life paths had been abruptly ended on account of his grandfather's interruption of their life cycle. He had killed them for his pleasure. The pleasure of his taste buds at that!

Ralphio wiped his tears and made a silent prayer for the souls of all those animals and requested Mother Gaia to help them reach their peaceful soul state in whatever dimension they were now.

As for his grandfather, he made another silent prayer to his soul to give up meat now, if he hadn't already. He was in 4D Ralphio knew now. Still alive but at what cost!

He opened his eyes as tears streamed from them and he looked out the window at the blue ball in space. What a beautiful planet it was. Ralphio smiled as the thought crossed his mind, pity the people there did not realize there was so much life teeming just outside their orbit.

He closed his eyes and put his head against the windowpane as he slowly drifted off to sleep, his mind unburdened with half-inherited memories of his grandfather. A slight knowing smile crossed his face as he entered the dream world.

...

There was fog all around, Ralphio seemed to be in the middle of a mountaintop, and lush green vegetation surrounded him everywhere he looked. From a distance, he saw a curvaceous figure of a woman clad in long flowy khakee robes. She seemed to be adorned with ornaments made of flowers and fruits. She came near him taking her time, took his hand and put the back of his hand on either of her eyes before joining her hands in a namaskaram before him.

Thank you for understanding she murmured to him just before she turned and left.

Ralphio did not get a good look at her face, her head being bowed down towards the ground. In his heart, however, he knew what Mother Gaia meant by this interaction. He knelt in gratitude to her and closed his eyes as a gentle breeze caressed his cheek. His life was complete.

...

Ralphio woke with a start, the bus rumbled as the lights flickered on and off, looked like it was time to take off again. He quickly took one last gaze at the twin Earths and he could swear on his wife's head that he got a wink back from them. He smiled as the bus got enveloped in darkness and before he could think about what was going to happen Ralphio was gone!

...

Similar to the first time, before he could think about what had happened, he was back at parking lot no.44 on Humanity Memorial Street when he saw the next batch of passengers line up with a ticket in hand waiting to board the bus.

"We hope you had a safe and enlightening journey. I'm Shin Stamprickle. Thank you for choosing Thought Travel for all your travel and education needs." Shin's voice echoed from the in-built speaker in the bus. Ralphio was brought back to reality as a child realized he had teleported and started to cry.

"Please find our travel catalogue below your seats. First people to book the next tour with us get 50% off…special discount for school children and senior citizens…."

Ralphio zoned out the rest of the words coming out of the microphone and took out his sketchbook. On it were two disfigured replicas of the twin Earths he had hurriedly managed to get. He was going to cherish this experience for a long long time. In fact, he was….

"Sir are you ready to get off?" a voice came from next to his ear as someone shook him gently. Ralphio turned his face to the left as Shin's wide smile on his pimply face came into view. "Sir we need to empty the bus now. The tour's over."

"Err, yes. Right. I'll just get off here then. Thank you for this tour" was all that Ralphio managed to say to Shin.

His heart was full but as always, his words were few.

"My wife will be waiting for me. I'll buy her favourite flowers on my way back. She was the one who insisted I go on this tour, you see" Ralphio said to Shin who had already moved on to the next row to wake up the senior citizen couple snoring together in perfect rhythm.

Petunias. Her favourite were petunias. Ralphio remembered. He got up as the vision of Mother Gaia carrying a petunia on her left ear came to his mind pulling a smile out of him like nothing in the past few months had.

What a day it had been. What a day.

THE LAST HOPE

THE LAST HOPE

-Rishabh Dubey 'Kridious'

Rishabh Dubey, better known by his pen-name 'Kridious', is an author and a musician based out of Mumbai, India. Kridious has several books to his name, including Novels spanning the realms of Science Fiction, Fantasy and others. Dubey is also a researcher and has published his research in both the fields of Science and Science Fiction.

A massive stroke of wind gushed through the dusty roads of what seemed like an abandoned and isolated town. It was though not as waste-clad as one would presume since the debris had either withered away or had become one with the stationary. There was no sign of any life anywhere. The absence of any traces of beings indicated how the place had long been deserted. A squirrel came out of a small opening to the sewer. It moved about for a while, searching for something to eat. The window pane that lay behind her slightly gave way to reveal a dark pair of eyes staring directly at the little animal. All of a sudden, the window slid open as a woman, with her face wrapped in cloth, jumped out towards the squirrel. She chased the animal for a while. Then, a large number of humans started barging out of the different structures and corners of the block. They were all wholly wrapped in rugged clothes and were all chasing the small squirrel. A riot began amid the road as more people kept joining and jumping on each other, beating each other down and trying to grab the squirrel.

Suddenly, the public address system attached to the posts started sounding a substantial and long Siren, the sound of which could've rendered anyone deaf. The vast mob immediately started dispersing in a terrified manner, trampling over a few who couldn't carry themselves well. The stampede left behind a few of them crippled, unable to reach back inside. The Siren went on for a few minutes and then became silent. No one was coming to help the fallen. The woman observed from her window-pane as the injured looked towards one side of the road with terrified expressions. They cried out for help, but no one listened. The winds started gaining pace. Everyone inside rushed further indoors. What followed was an enormous dust storm. It continued for some time, causing no conspicuous damage to the buildings and other structures. They had apparently become used to it and had shed whatever they could have. As soon as the storm subsided, the woman slowly walked back to the window. She was shivering as she dared to look at the ones who had been left behind. They were all dead, and their bodies had turned black as if charred.

"Three more lost… They could've been fed to the scavengers…" said the young and muscular man standing on the window pane beside her. She slowly turned back and walked inside. She then slid open a wooden cover on the ground, revealing a stairwell. Walking down, she reached a dark and small basement.

"Aasha…" she whispered as her sound reverberated.

"Aasha…" she repeated louder after hearing no reply. A small warm hand came and clasped hers. She took out a solar torch from her coat pocket and switched it on. The light revealed a little girl sitting beside her in the dark. She was wearing half-torn and saggy clothes but had nothing covering her face.

"How many times have I told you to cover your face?" the woman said in anger, as she looked for cloth in the little room.

"But… I don't need it you told me…" Aasha said.

"No… but the world needs one on you or else they'd be afraid of you…" the woman said as she picked up a ripped piece of cloth and started wrapping it around

Aasha's face. "I feel Hungry, Mother..." the young girl said.

"I know... The storm hit before we could get any food. I'd be going out again soon. Did you finish the water bottle I gave you? Preserve it. Asmit is acting weirder every day. He might not let many take their share of water next time..." the woman said. A rattling sound started coming from above immediately followed by someone saying "SCAVENGERS...". The woman quickly pushed the child to a corner of the basement.

"No matter what happens... DO NOT MAKE A NOISE... AND DO NOT COME OUT..." she said while shutting her lamp off. She then climbed out of the basement and shut the lid, putting broken rubbles to cover it up. Everyone had gathered near the windows again. Outside, two black motorcycles had stopped, each ridden by one person. They both were completely covered in grey bodysuits which extended as helmets over their faces. They took out some electronic devices from their backpacks and put them on the road. Inside, everybody had picked up a piece of wood, knife, sword or any broken piece of equipment they could've used as a weapon.

"I have never seen such scavengers before..." said a young man standing at a corner of the building in which the woman stood.

The two riders were doing something with a signal dish on the ground. One of them walked up to the charred bodies of the people who had died earlier. The other one said looking at their device "Radiation is low here... So, is the groundwater… We can stay here but cannot extract for long."

"Radiation is low… No Kidding… These are freshly burnt… We should expect company" the other one said while gazing at the charred bodies.

"Guess what… this place reported merely seven hundred thousand cases at peak…" the one sitting at the computer said.

"They must have migrated to the camps long ago… Damn, I feel hungry…" the other one said.

"Grab me that bar when you take one for yourself. I would do a pulse mapping of the place. We then move ahead. Sounds cool?"

"They have food…" said the muscular man standing inside the building. The woman looked at him and whispered: "Please do not do anything foolish Asmit…"

"Sarita… Why do you fear fights so much? Don't you have that little girl below to feed? Feed her well, or she'd become too weak… and possibly scavengers' food…" Asmit replied.

Sarita looked back at him with anger. He then gestured towards some people to come forward with their weapons. He reached inside his pocket and took out a revolver.

"Asmit… Where did you?" Sarita questioned.

"It is just the two of them… We apprehend quick and steal whatever they carry." Asmit said. "And what about them?" Sarita questioned.

"We leave their fate outside… Storm or the Scavengers… whichever comes first." Asmit replied. He then quickly opened the door, pointing the gun towards them. They were both startled. A crowd gathered behind him as he slowly walked forward.

"You are not from around here… What brings you?" Asmit questioned.

The two riders had both stood up and raised their hands slightly above their waists to show that they were both harmless.

"We are not here to take anything from you… We just wish to scan the red zones for habitable land… And then we'd be gone…" the rider next to the computer on the ground said.

"Hahahaha" Asmit laughed as the others behind him followed.

"What decade are you living in? There are only red zones here… Here… if you're unarmed, you're a settler. Or else, you are a scavenger…" he continued.

"Kill them and take their stuff." A man behind Asmit said. "Yes…" many others followed.

"Are you a scavenger? Well… We come a long distance from the green zone…" said the other rider, as instant silence prevailed. They all looked at them in awe.

"You're lying… There is nothing like that anymore… We were abandoned years ago…" Asmit said. "No… we do… he is not lying. We're from the Federation…" the rider near the computer said.

Everyone started discussing amongst each other after that revelation. Then, there was a gunshot. Asmit was holding his revolver up in the air. He pulled the revolver's hammer to load another bullet and pointed his gun at the rider near the computer.

"The Federation is a myth… And those who speak of myths… Must die…" Asmit said furiously. Suddenly, a loud voice was heard from inside "NOOO". It was Sarita. She came running in front of Asmit.

"If what they say is true… we can find the haven we once longed for…" Sarita said.

"Get out my way… I cannot waste bullets on the weak…" Asmit said. All of a sudden, another gunshot was heard. This one, not from Asmit's gun. A man standing behind him had been shot in his leg. They all looked towards the other side of the road to see shadowed figures rising above the horizon. They were all riding horses.

"SCAVENGERS… RUNNN…" screamed one of them as they started escaping back inside. Sarita had run towards the fallen man. She tried to seal his bullet wound with her arm, trying to find a piece of cloth to tie over it. One of the riders came to her and said "It's a waste… He'd die. Save yourself…"

Sarita looked up. Her eyes were desperate. She took off the cloth wrapped on her face and measured it. It was too small to be torn in half. She wrapped it around the injured leg of the man. One of the two riders pressed a button on their helmet, which slid open to reveal another glass coating beneath it. The rider's face was visible. She was a woman.

"Let me help you get inside…" she said as she began to help Sarita drag the wounded man inside the building beside her. Meanwhile, the other rider was busy packing their equipment. After doing that, they pressed a few buttons on the electronic device attached to their wrist. They went close to the motorcycles and stood beside them. The scavengers had reached the spot. The heavy man sitting on a horse at the centre stepped down.

"My My… Someone give him a fancy-dress award…" he said, as the others behind him laughed.

The woman rider walked outside. Her face was still visible.

"We've got a pair have we now?" the man said. "Who are you?" the woman rider asked.

"My apologies… My name is Mandeep… Though, with all the love that is due, around here they call me Rakshasa…" he said as he punched the woman in her gut.

"Hey… We want no trouble… We are here for the Federation's work. We're under oath and are protected…" the other rider said.

"The Federation you say… Vali…" Mandeep said as another man stepped down off his horse. He carried a substantial automatic rifle in his hand and a long knife on his side.

"They are from the Federation… I have heard of it before… much before the bright-night. You were one of them… those fighting for the cure… Weren't they Vali?" he said as Vali replied, "Yes Sir…"

"It was because of a war of wealth that you and your likes waged that humankind was destroyed… My family… All our families… Everything. We lost. And with humankind… we lost our humanity too… And now you shall suffer a worse fate. Tie them up… A Man and a Woman… They would satisfy both the of hungers of my men…" he said as his men stepped down and rushed with ropes.

"Don't go too close to my brother… He's positive…" the woman said. Mandeep turned around.

"Brother… So, your siblings I see. He's positive…" Mandeep said as he made a gesture towards Vali. The latter brought a small leather satchel to him. He took out a shiny metallic from inside and loaded it inside his pistol.

"The thing I have put in my gun is a raider-tech from the days of the civil war. When the ballistics of the world had expired, and the human race still survived… Millions of these were made after the bright-night. The weapon of domination has never been the one to inflict the most harm. It is the one to inflict the most fear. The virus, in its most lethal mutation, was frozen with its carrier blood in these bullet capsules. Fear… The weapon of the Gods… Well, why am I telling you all this? Let's see how positive your brother is…" Mandeep said, pointing his gun at the rider. Suddenly, the Sirens started sounding.

"It cannot be… So, soon…" Mandeep, alarmed, said nervously. The scavengers behind him started climbing their horses.

"Fools… we cannot escape the storm… Find refuge inside… We would deal with them later… Come on" he said as the scavengers stepped down again. Mandeep and his men started trying to get the horses inside but to no resolve. The openings were too small to fit them. They then abandoned the horses and rushed inside the building where Asmit and Sarita were there.

"Everyone move inside… Whoever moves a muscle will be thrown out in the storm. Everyone other than my men are to drop whatever they hold…" Mandeep said in a commanding tone. They all followed his command. Then, Asmit spoke up "Mandeep… We told you… You'd find nothing here. We have been looted many a time by the eastern scavengers."

"We still happen to find you every time, don't we? Don't push me to take more of you. We'd search… If we don't find something… we take one of you. If we do find… I would take you this time…" Mandeep said. His men dispersed with their solar-torches trying to find anything of value. They grabbed all the little water containers they saw and collected them.

Meanwhile, the two riders sat in a corner on the floor near Sarita. The latter was trying to mitigate the pain of the man who had been injured earlier. The second rider also pushed a button on his helmet to reveal his glass-covered face.

"Hi! My name is Abdul… That's my elder sister Inaya. We were not expecting… so much turbulence here…" the man said.

"Hey… I am Sarita" Sarita said, as she kept gazing at the rubble she had earlier kept above the lid.

Abdul followed her eyes and observed meticulously to see the small wooden latch.

"What's down there?" Abdul asked.

"Nothing… What? Where?" Sarita said anxiously.

"Abdul has the habit of troubling people. Ignore him. Why did you save this guy?" Inaya asked. "We… Kill. We have been killing only. For once, I wanted to feel what it is like to save someone. But I couldn't…" Sarita said as she left the wounded man's hand. It fell down. He wasn't breathing.

"It is a survivor's world right now… Tell me. When was the last time you ate?" Inaya asked. "It has been more than a week…" Sarita replied.

"We have food in our backpacks outside. We will give it to you… Don't share. We only have one person's worth extra, and we would want to give it to someone who believes in saving for a change." Inaya said.

"But it is going to rot and burn in the storm outside…" Sarita said. "There is no storm… I triggered the Siren." Abdul said.

"What? You did? But… I would just need a little… not for myself…" Sarita said.

Abdul turned towards the rubble again. "For the one who is down there… Your child?" he asked.

"Not mine… She… I found her. I adopted her…" Sarita said. Just as she did, a scavenger tripped over the rubble. He fell down and saw the latch.

"Sir… There is a lid here…" he said as he moved the rubble away. They opened the lid. Sarita began tightening her fist out of worry while Abdul and Inaya tried to calm her down.

"There is nothing down there…" Sarita screamed.

"Let's see…" Vali said and went inside. There came a screaming sound of the young girl. Then, Vali came out, grabbing her in his arms.

"We have found a hidden treasure…" Vali said.

"Dessert today men…" Mandeep said. He then raised his gun towards Sarita.

"I have said to never hide anything from me… You shall get a reward for this…" Mandeep said, as he turned his gun towards Aasha and pulled the trigger. The bullet pierced through her shoulder. The little girl screamed in pain and fainted. Sarita got up and was held back by Abdul and Inaya. The scavengers were pointing their guns at them all.

"Reminds me… Why hasn't the storm struck yet? Vali… Go outside and check…" Mandeep said.

"Me? Sir? Outside?" Vali asked.

"Don't make me repeat myself…" Mandeep said. Vali asked a few men to follow him and went out. Mandeep walked towards Asmit. "You lie and lie and lie…" Mandeep said, moving his gun around Asmit's face. He turned around over his shoulder and asked Asmit's own people "What should I do with him?". Simultaneously, Asmit slowly drew his pistol. He immediately grabbed hold of Mandeep's neck and turned him away from himself, pointing the gun at his head.

"I would kill your boss…" Asmit said. Everyone began laughing.

"You know why they laugh? You kill one head of a Rakshasa, and another takes its place…" Mandeep said as he threw Asmit over his shoulder. Utilising that distraction, Abdul and Inaya took out their own guns from their suits and started shooting at the scavengers. Mandeep got shot in his right foot. There was an all-out battle. Suddenly, Asmit picked up his pistol and shot Mandeep in his head. The scavengers were shaken. They were immediately overpowered by the people around them and rendered weaponless within seconds. Vali came inside again with his men and was shot in his leg by Abdul.

"Seems like the head of this Rakshasa was without brain… The one that replaces (turned to Vali), hopefully, HAS a brain. Return now… There is no storm coming… The alarm was fake. We'd let you live." Inaya said.

Vali asked his scavengers to retreat. They went out, climbed their horses and started back in the direction they came from. As soon as they did, Asmit said "Everybody… Grab all the plastic you can. We need to wrap the little girl. None of her blood or body remains here…"

"What are you doing? She would bleed out…" Sarita said. Asmit turned his pistol towards her.

"You stay out of it… We're not going to die of the thing we have successfully avoided for so long…"

Asmit said with determination.

"No… SHE IS IMMUNE…" Sarita said. Silence prevailed in the entire building. "What… How can that be?" Asmit asked.

Sarita lashed out in tears "Yes… I found her… Post the bright-night… When those raiders unleashed the civil war and created fomites in every possible corner of the country… I was a health worker for one side. We were sent to look for survivors. I initially didn't know what they had planned for them. Eventually, I learnt that the immune was too big a threat to them… To all of them. They were ruthlessly killing them all. That's what happens when you have cowards giving commands… But I found her. She was merely an infant… covered in too many bodies of the dead. All who died of the virus. Yet, she lived. I hid her from them all… And ran. Became a scavenger for as long as I could, but kept moving till we got tired. Then we became settlers with you… But she would never be infected by the virus. Let me heal her… or she would die of the wound…" Sarita said. Everyone was shocked to hear her.

"The risk is too high…" Asmit said as he pulled the hammer and started moving the gun towards Aasha. "Hey, Big Man…" Abdul said, trying to intercept him. Asmit, startled, shot Abdul twice in the neck. He kept pulling the trigger, but his barrel was empty.

"Noooooooo… Brother…" Inaya said as she rushed to her brother. Sarita ran to have a look at Aasha. He took his last few heavy breaths and then passed away. Inaya lost her senses and ran towards Asmit. She pushed him down and pointed her gun to his face and screamed at the top of her voice "I AM GOING TO KILL YOU…". Everyone grabbed some or the other thing and assembled around Inaya.

"STOP IT… PLEASE… NO MORE KILLING…" Sarita screamed.

"Why are we humans, so hell-bent on just thinking of ourselves… First, the Pandemic… Then the war for the cure… We bloody launched nuclear missiles at each other. I don't know why we call the darkest of all nights as the bright-night. Worse is what followed… a species already divided into so many warring nations was even further divided. 'Every Man for Himself' they said. What did it give us? WHAT DID WE GET FROM ANY OF IT? LOOK AT US… We have destroyed everything… and we keep on destroying each day we extend our hands to take away from another… rather than spreading them to help another. They say a virus defeated us… No… Not a virus. We alone defeat our own bloody selves…" Sarita said as she tried to stop Aasha's bleeding. Inaya got up and kept her gun back inside. She was still furious. She walked to Sarita and got down on her knees. She then took a small tube out of the belt strap she was wearing and applied the jelly-like liquid inside on Aasha's wound.

"That's an instant coagulant. She won't bleed out. But we've to get her bullet out soon…" Inaya said. Sarita kept crying. "I'm sorry about your brother." Even Asmit burst into tears as he sat up. "What have I done…" he said to himself. Everyone kept their weapons down and sat in circles around Inaya and Sarita.

"Can you save her?" Sarita asked.

"Yes… And she can save us all…" Inaya said as the Siren started sounding again. "Is this you again?" asked a woman sitting beside them.

"No… This time it is for real… I have to leave immediately…" Inaya said as she lifted Aasha over her shoulder and started walking outside.

"My brother's body… I would come for it…" she said as she walked to her bike. She kept Aasha over it and sat behind her.

"WAIT…" came Asmit's voice as he came running out with a water bottle. "That's the last of my water… Take it…" he said.

"Then keep it for yourself… You would need it. And wait (grabbed the two backpacks from the ground). Take these… Share the food and water with everyone. And, my brother's guns… They hang by his sides. This time… Use them to protect your people…" Inaya said as she started her bike and moved forward.

After covering a little distance ahead, she tried to establish a connection with her base. "Foxtrot… Come in… This is Dr Inaya Rehman… Can you hear me?" she said over the radio.

"Yes, Dr Inaya… We can hear you loud and clear…" a woman's sound came from the radio.

"I am reporting from the heart of the north-western red-zone… in the province of Awadh. Requesting relocation to nearest safe bunker due to incoming storm." Inaya said.

"Finding the nearest location for you, Doctor. Is Dr Abdul still with you or have you already parted your ways for mapping?"

Inaya took a pause. She then sighed and said with a shivering voice: "Dr Abdul was killed in action due to scavenger raids".

"I am sorry to hear that…"

"One more request… Please make sure there is an infirmary at the bunker since I carry a wounded with me…" Inaya said. "A wounded… Who?"

"It is a little girl. She has a bullet wound. But she has to live. She is Immune to the virus…" Inaya said. "What? Immune?"

"Yes… We have found a Naturally Immune Subject…" Inaya said.

"What? Can you confirm that you said "Naturally Immune Subject?" the woman on the other side of the communicator said.

Inaya looked at Aasha. She controlled the tears dripping down her eyes for her brother, concealed the pain that was still fresh and was engulfing her heart, gave in to the small spark of faith that the little girl had revived inside her, smiled and said "Yes… We have found… Hope…"

THE PROOF

THE PROOF!

-Sapna Katti

Sapna Katti is a postgraduate in Electronics from Karnataka University, Dharwad. Sci-fi has been the theme of interest from the beginning; rather than the complex details of scientific and technological inventions, she is intrigued by its effect on the human psyche. Her stories have different themes like humanoids and their consequences in day-to-day life, brain transfer and degradation of value systems by it (futuristic), nanotechnology etc. She has written many sci-fi fiction stories in Kannada. Her story "He She and It" won 3rd prize in a national-level sci-fi story writing competition held by the renowned magazine "Science Reporter" in 2021 and was published in the April 2022 issue of the same. Around 20 non-sci-fi stories have been published in many Kannada magazines.; interested in translating good sci-fi stories from English to Kannada as well. Bringing out her anthology of stories is her dream.

"Manav Manav" Yash shouted as he entered the huge basement of his laboratory situated in the east of the Jaintia Hills district amidst the beautiful greenery of Meghalaya. Before even Yash could hear the echo of his own voice, Manav called right from his back "I'm here sir". Yash was scared out of his wits.

"What the hell…Why don't you make a bit of sound while walking" Yash said irritably.

"The soft pads under my feet are specially designed not to make any sound. Otherwise, can you imagine sir the noise I would create along with the chilling screams of bats in this laboratory? "

"I know I know" Yash shouted, "I don't need preaching from a robot", but strangely he felt hurt.

Actually, Yash always had this doubt that the robot designed by the 'The Pioneers' IT company in collaboration with the government had some chips engraved in it to create a sense of frustration in him so that he would push himself hard to achieve the results. So, sometimes without reason, he would get upset with Manav. Some other times he would embrace Manav tightly and say "Well done my boy"!

Who did he have but the machine to love or to vent his anger anyway? He thought at times 'Should I leave all my property to Manav after my death?' and moments later he would have a hearty laugh at his foolishness. Yash was getting a fat salary and a huge annual grant for his research work from the government as he was the best living chiropterologist in India. All hopes were pinned on him since the Indian government had decided to take the study of the link between the Bt Cov virus found in bats and the human COVID virus very seriously after the outbreak of the pandemic in 2020. It lasted for two years, getting mutated three times and claimed the lives of millions of humans throughout the world. Incidentally, its second wave had killed Yash's father who lived in his native village of Kerala alone, after his retirement as a school teacher. The death of the only loving soul he had shaken Yash completely. When he decided to become a chiropterologist many of his relatives raised their brows though they knew him as a kid who always enjoyed doing things differently from his peers. If his friends would go to fairs and cinemas on holidays, he would go to nearby woods alone, sit by the river, eat packets of biscuits and count the trees around there until evening! Soon he could recognize almost all the species of trees by their leaves, jungle birds by their chirps and flowers by their smells. Even he named the variety of bats found there as Shriek Samba, Chilling Chinnu, Biggy Brat etc., based on their strange high pitch screams. His friends had started calling him 'Batman'. His desire to study the flying mammal originated from there or from a strong will to find a cure to the flu to which his father subsequently succumbed, he himself did not know.

"Sir your coffee" Manav placed the steaming mug on the table. The coffee looked as dark as the bats ranging from a few centimetres to two metres in width, lying lifeless in big white jars arranged in rows there. Their large wings with bone-like fingers stretched over them looked like broken masts of a wrecked ship in the sea.

Each time Yash felt that he had found a clue to his theory - certain genetic changes made in the DNA of Pterous and Rousettus species of bats can make them impossible to host COVID viruses- his test would fail as viruses would have mutated by that time. Then he had to induce new changes again in the artificial DNA created by him before implanting it in the host.

Nevertheless, each failure made him more determined and more passionate to achieve success. He would often say proudly to Manav "My father did not name me Yash without a reason" and each time Manav would respond, though mechanically, "Sir your eyes sparkle when you speak of your father" and Yash would be pleased. He started studying all 2200 varieties of bats found throughout the globe with new vigour and had become an expert on their food habits and habitats, their adaptability and reproduction pattern by the year 2030; Today he could call himself both as chiropterologist and a virologist.

He opened the mailbox for the fourth time that day as it was the only link left between the world over there and him.

Though he would be often fishing for appreciation and love in the mails, he would shrug his shoulders and say to the staring machine "Just checking for current 'virus scenario' across the globe, that's all" and the robot would say "Sure sir, now shall I bring you a cup of lemon tea?" But today there was a rare mail; from his aunt Neenakka who was herself a scientist at a defence laboratory in Kerala. Yash suddenly began to feel the familiar feeling of uneasiness in the pit of his stomach which he always felt towards her, though she was the lady who financed him during his college days when his father could not afford the fees. Sometimes she would send them the groceries and medicines etc. But Yash as a teenager would feel "Why does Aunty not make a phone call even once? Why she never visits us?" He detested the feeling of an orphan he would get each time he received money from her. He had refused to take her money once his scholarships began.

No blessings, no hi, hello, the business-like letter read: "The long fruitless research and loneliness have turned the scientist in you into a man against the creatures themselves. Do you know that the indiscriminate killing of the bats is leading to the destruction of mangroves along coastal lines here? Don't you hear the cries of helpless rice and tea farmers who have lost their crops since you are killing thousands of pest eaters? I feel very sad to note that you are no more a crusader against the virus but a mindless killer, that's all". Yash began to feel furious and started to shiver uncontrollably. Manav immediately rushed to him and carried him to bed and began putting cold ice packs on his sweat-dripping forehead. Later Yash wondered why each time he felt like crying, droplets appeared on his forehead and not in his eyes.

The bat lying on his table was huge, almost three metres in width, 'but the helplessness and pain in his black round eyes do not suit his large size' Yash thought as he began to take its rectal swabs. Bat began to scream loudly and it was not a usual ultrasound echo squeak but the cry of a hurt animal and its decibel power filled Yash's ears with pain. The whole basement echoed its scream. "You damn creature!" he shouted loudly and gave a sleep-inducing injection to it. Bat gave violent shrugs before losing consciousness.

Manav who was watching everything silently now started putting back the bat with its human-like soft hands in the chamber and waited there to give it fish food after it woke up. When Yash also returned having finished his favourite 'protein sandwich dinner' Manav began to wrap his arm with a strap to measure his blood pressure and pulse rate as that was a daily routine.

"Sir I just read an article in a journal; it says -bats do not carry most of the zoonotic viruses. There are too many species of them; hence more tests on them - also it's too easy to catch bats, isn't it sir?" Manav suddenly asked. Yash smiled as he knew that the robot was filled with relevant information on bats by its makers to give Yash a feeling of 'scientific discussion' with it. But somehow today he did not feel like answering.

"Sir the probability theory says, the more the things tested more will be the results. So, how do you know that the rarely tested cobras and pythons do not contain viruses?" Manav seemed insistent.

"Don't teach me probability theory. Bats' roosts are near human habitats and hence the higher chance of infection from them."

"Okay sir, one more thing. The article says -that bats are not just protein packs available naturally for man but are the creations of God himself- Who is God, sir?"

Yash just could not answer him as he choked with laughter.

"Sir keep laughing ... your blood pressure is dropping into the normal range as you started laughing, God must be a really great person sir.... he made your pressure go down without the medicine," Manav remarked matter-of-factly.

"No, God is somebody .... who makes me, my hard work, and everything in this world including you irrelevant, because he is supposed to do miracles with one swing of his magic wand"?

Again, Yash laughed wryly.

"Then why don't you request him for some help regarding your research sir?"

"Okay, Manav, now enough of the discussion about immaterial things. I have a web conference to attend. Please don't disturb me for an hour."

As he logged in to his 'face2face' meeting site, professor Anurag Byanarjee, head of the 'scientific growth review committee' set up by the central government was already there. He did not wave his hand to Yash like always but started his discussion with a grim note.

"Yash, you must know that it is becoming harder year after year to pursue government to sanction your research the annual grants as there are no substantial developments in your 'genetic changes' theory of bats."

"Sir but is it not established long back that Ebola viruses were hosted by bats?"

"That's true, but it's also equally true that millions of people in Africa, Pacific and Indian ocean islands co-exist with bats without the overspill of diseases"

"Sir, but we fear most what we understand least. So, let me study more of them and test…."

"Yash…" Mr Byanarjee interrupted "Let it be of anything, every quest reaches a stage when one wonders 'Is it a quest for the good of mankind or has it become just a personal obsession?' Is it not high time you pondered over this? After all, bats are not worthless to be just guinea pigs for your experiments"

'Now he is getting philosophical!' Yash thought as he began to feel irritated. He finished his talk abruptly and walked towards the window to light a cigarette. The scratch made by a dying bat on his cheek looked even deeper in the dim light that came from the road above. He just stood there watching his long shadow getting cut short by the high compound wall around the building. Suddenly his eyes gleamed with a strange vengeance as he paced towards the sleeping bat and began to inject a chemical into it.

The morning had not matured yet by the time Yash woke from his sleep; looming clouds in the eastern sky looked like blood-soaked cotton balls to him. As he sipped dark strong coffee, the stains of last night's bad dreams began to clear and he decided he needed a brisk walk outside to make his blood a bit warmer. Manav followed him like a soldier.

As they came to the ground behind the building a strange smell filled Yash's nose and there was a silence that felt like ash-covered coal; looking white and cold but ready to turn into flames anytime! Then there was a loud screeching sound that seemed to come from behind the trees. His blood turned cold as he stood staring at the mammoth bat almost the size of his house coming towards him slowly. Even in the dizziness, he felt at that moment, he realized that his worst fears had come true. The constant chemical reactions done on its DNA had increased its size by hundreds of times and one stroke of its wing would be sufficient to kill a man. He signalled Manav to bring his pistol but the bat attacked in a split second and knocked him down. Blood oozed from his head as he hit a huge rock.

Then the gigantic mammal flew away. Manav tried all the techniques to revive his heartbeat but in vain. It knew from stored memory that all vampire bats that tasted human blood once would come back to their prey. He ran quickly to the attic and got hold of a Ruger SP102 pistol and ran back to the ground. As anticipated, the bat which was flying in circles in the sky, dived instantly at Manav, but the robot was quicker. The subsonic bullet hit the mammal straight in the throat and it collapsed on the ground with a great thud.

Manav sat beside Yash's body and called Professor Byanarjee "Sir this project is over. Sadly, Dr Yash Menon was killed by his creation. But sir he is not a failure, he did achieve the genetic changes in bats and his death is proof of it…." Professor Byanarjee rubbed the screen of his mobile with his hand in disbelief at what he saw on it. Manav's hard lines of jaw seemed to soften, anguish seemed to peep in his voice as he spoke and his white chalklike cheeks slowly turned pink.

"Oh my God!" he said "Yes, certainly his theory was a success, Manav. Anyway, Yash has never ceased to astonish me with his great achievements. Knowingly or unknowingly he did a miracle and I am looking at it now. We are coming there to fetch you" Byanarjee whispered slowly.

UNHEARD
SCREAMS

UNHEARD SCREAMS

-Kshama Gautam

Kshama Gautam belongs to Kota, Rajasthan. Besides being a writer of fiction, she is a poet, translator and theatre artist. She is an English Teacher by profession. She has written several short stories along with a book for children under the title, "Daisy's Diary". She has translated five Science fiction books so far, written by esteemed authors.

"Calm down, it'll be all fine," Anu said hiding her fear and blanketing her face with forced ease.

"No, I don't think so, everything has finished! Our future, our life... everything! You understand?" Roohi was not prepared to get anything.

"Did you hear they said that we are going to be safe......?" Anu again tried to console her.

Kota City used to be full of energetic students. Illuminated with bright faces of young boys and girls, was looking like a haunted place. One could grasp River Chambal's melancholic whispers from afar. Stalls, where, from early morning, students would crowd like bees over honeycomb, were locked. The whole city sank in despair. No sounds of horns and hawkers. Only nature seemed to be delighted as there was no smoke and no harmful gases. Nature was healing itself and some curse on human beings was in process. There was something in the air that restricted humans from walking out.

It had been almost one month now and the building was almost empty. Sometimes they both could even feel their own course of breathing, their heartbeats. Their shadows gave them a realization of two more people. Dark, horrible as well as horrified, two countenances. Ten days ago, all children who shared that same building with them had been sent to their hometowns by authorities. They belonged to Kolkata, only two remained there and there seemed no arrangement for them to reach their hometown. The hostel's kitchen was closed. Roads were deserted and shops were shut. What to eat and how to survive? The corridor which appeared very narrow before a month now seemed a never-ending path. The walls looked extra huge with locked doors. The Peepul tree, behind the hostel building, waved its branches to make the environment creepier. The drawings, mischievous girls once made on the walls never appeared so animated. Roohi especially avoided going out at night in the corridor. One night she dreamt of a man covered with so many thorns on his body running towards her. He wore a red cloak. She ran and ran on the empty road. She screamed but no one could hear. Then all of a sudden, the man stretched his arm to grab her. She could feel the pricks on her bare skin. She woke up with a shriek. Sweat drops drenched her whole body.

Anu and Roohi were students of 11th standard. They were from West Bengal and were studying advanced lectures for fighting IIT entrance examination. Anu was a pretty girl with a sweet voice and fair complexion. She always kept a broad smile on her face. Her hair was short and she wore spectacles. Unlike Anu, Roohi was tall and had a dark complexion. Roohi was a little impatient and restless by nature. Her big eyes and pitch-black long hair were enough to attract anyone. Anu was able to manage the circumstances. On the contrary, Roohi was on tenterhooks and could not handle the furry of time.

"These walls will swallow me Anu and this ceiling will fall upon us at night....and you know.... that will be fine... I want to die rather than to be alive like this " She said. Anu collected her courage once more.

"Forget it.... ok, state, what would you have for lunch? Noodles or bread? And here.... see we have some ground nuts too." Anu articulated. But Roohi was not present at the scene. She was gazing at the windowpane with a blank face. She was afraid of sleeping at night. She was sure that nightmares would disturb her.

"Anu....listen to me.... close this window. they say it can spread through the air and when we breathe, we may also be infected... Anu I want to live... I want to be an engineer...." nothing could relax Roohi and Anu, this time burst into tears after listening to her. She buried her face beneath the pillow and sobbed. Roohi remained untouched, still sitting and gazing out of the window.

COVID-19 ruled the world. So, many people stuck wherever they were. No work, no commuting, even no walking on the roads. It was more pathetic for children who were studying far from their native places. It fell upon day labourers' like a bad omen. All over India, thousands of labourers work in Metropolitan cities leaving their families behind in small villages. When the Government decided to stop all activities, the poor became poorer. Poverty-stricken people imagined committing suicide. They save every single penny to serve their families. Some of them decided to go to their home towns walking hundreds of kilometres. But then the borders of the states were sealed and thus threw them into despair. Pregnant women were terrified to give birth to their babies. The havoc of COVID-19 had drawn everyone's life to a close. Hospitals were crowded. There were no sufficient beds and the lack of nursing staff as well as doctors was another giant issue. There spread a tribulation and anguish. Roohi was not like this earlier. She behaved perfectly before ten days when so many other students were staying there. She was chirpy as usual. But now she began to overreact. Anu never told her parents about this change but the last call of her mother induced a doubt into her head. Her mother Prabha talked to Anu then to confirm. Roohi was the only child of her parents. They were also helpless. They would call up here and there all the time. They had put in all possible efforts.

"Is she alright? Anu I'm her mom, I can sniff something else in Roohi, tell me. O, God, what's happening to my daughter?" She panicked. Anu affirmed that she was fine but a little worried regarding her studies and future. But it was not that simple. Roohi was going through the blues of separation, a long period of isolation. Misery hovered over them and only some audacious people could face that situation.

How to tell her mother that Roohi wore a mask even in the room? She washed her hands almost every fifteen minutes and gargled now and then. Anu was tired of making her understand that she was safe. She would wake up from sleep twice or thrice to confirm that the door was shut. Sometimes she would open and close it again and again.

They had a few things in store to eat. Roohi avoided eating and this made Anu more worried. At night monstrous sounds scared them. One night it seemed to them as if someone was unlocking the next door, they turned into stones. Someone laughed out loudly and knocked on their door too. They experienced hallucinations. Somehow Anu knew it was not real. But Roohi encountered the angst. The anxiety of losing her life. They were fed up with eating noodles daily.

"Roohi....get up now... it's 8 o'clock" Anu woke her up. There was no reply.

"Roohi.!" She went to her bed and touched her cheek.

"O God, she has a fever," Anu murmured and rushed to the cupboard to take a pill to reduce fever.

"Roohi. Dear get up. I've prepared tea. Have something with tea and then take this tablet you have a fever I guess." Anu spoke.

"what? Fever? See I knew it would kill me. This virus will kill me. I told you...hey you...stay away from me. Don't touch me. And where is your mask? You better go to another room...leave me alone. I am going to die soon!" Roohi screamed.

Anu was sure that it was a normal fever that Roohi might have caught out of fright. Moreover, it was not so high temperature. Roohi could not tackle it and rushed to the stove. Then she started boiling water.

"I'll breathe in the steam. Don't ever call a doctor; he will behave like I'm going to kill him. I don't like this type of comportment. They will send me to quarantine. I would rather die here...you listen, don't touch me."

"But Roohi...please don't assume that you have that infection, you don't have a cough and cold. I know the symptoms." Anu tried her best to make her return to her senses. Now it seemed unbearable. Roohi was going through delirium. Her hands were trembling.

"Anu...look at me...I have produced red rashes all over my body be little keen to see. " Roohi said uneasily.

"Roohi I guess you should rest. I can't see anything on your skin. You're alright, trust me, dear." Anu could not control it now. This condition of Roohi almost murdered her. Roohi, inside the room, was breathing in steam. Then she bathed for a long time. Afterwards, she washed the floor and closed both the windows. She opened the cupboard and caressed her books and notebooks. She then stood with folded hands in front of Goddess Durga's little statue. She chanted some mantras. Tears rolled down her cheeks. Anu rushed outside of the room and cried a lot. Then something flashed in her head and granted her courage. She remembered a Psychotherapist who once came to their coaching centre to counsel the students. He must be a great help at this time. She searched and found his details. Dr Dhananjaya was the name.

Counsellor and Psychotherapist Dr Dhananjaya was a popular name in Kota. Dhananjaya was an impressive personality with six feet of height and a fair complexion. People, with Psychological problems, would feel relaxed only by conversing with him. He would pay a call to different educational institutions to meet especially teenagers and listen to their problems regarding diverse issues. In his late thirties, Dr Dhananjaya was loved by students as well as others in Kota and outside the city. Anu dialled his phone number.

"Yes...? Yes, speaking. tell me..." the voice of a male was heard from the other end which appeared very mollifying to Anu.

"Sir, I know you...my name is Anu. do you remember coming to our institute?"

Anu hesitated a bit to speak.

'aa. I usually visit various institutes, dear. come to the point. just explain your requirements. Do you want to ask something?" Dr Dhananjaya asked so politely that Anu could not control her tears. She regained her guts and began to speak.

"sir. My friend and I are alone in this hostel. All our companions left for their hometowns ten days ago....it was all fine earlier but all of a sudden my friend Roohi started behaving abnormally" Anu said.

"so...ok, how do you say she is abnormal? Did you notice some weird conduct of hers? Or she may be merely missing her parents"

"N-no, sir...oh, I mean yes sir. She is extremely horrified taking this certain infection. I know her. She is not the kind of girl who misses her parents to be sick...actually sir, she has a misconception that she has been infected by this disease and she is unable to handle this all going on nowadays!" Anu gathered her heartbeats and Dhananjaya could feel her agony.

"OK...calm down. She will be fine. Let me talk to her when you see she is comfortable there is nothing to worry about."

The doctor's voice soothed her. She went back into the room to see Roohi, curled in a corner, horrified.

"Roohi....dear take this pill with tea and you'll be fine. Ok. I assure you please take this pill for me. " Anu pleaded. Roohi took the tablet but refused to go to bed. She then forced Anu to wear a mask and gloves then after a long period of convincing Anu could make her sleep.

In the evening Roohi was better. Anu told her that someone was there to help her. He was a counsellor and she made her remember his visit to the institute. Anu told her that he wanted to talk to her. First Roohi hesitated but afterwards, on her friend's request, she was convinced to have words with Dhananjaya.

It took around five days and seven sets of conversations. The magical words of the doctor worked amazingly. Anu did not know what Dhananjaya spoke to Roohi in every session. She only saw a sparkle of hope in Roohi's eyes. She began to eat, even though she would walk in the corridor while talking to Dhananjaya. She would study as well. There was no more terror and nightmares. No mask-wearing inside the room. She let the fresh air come from the windows. She would listen to her favourite music. It was a wonderful change. Diseases must not snatch the power of self-healing. They must not overpower the strength of God. A man is mortal but his life is in the hands of that almighty. Anu did not know how it became possible that her friend was turning normal, what was that which Dhananjaya had thrown out of her brain. Is our mind being that brawny to make us ill or to throw us into delirium? We must control our brain to function properly. We should not let it harm ourselves. Anu understood the value of life and the value of self-controlling. She contemplated about Roohi. She was certain that Roohi would never be feeble in future. COVID-19 has taught so many lessons. Lessons of life as well as relations.

Roohi regained her vitality. Anu told Roohi's parents about this. Her parents were grateful. They thanked Dr Dhananjaya from the core of their heart. The doctor said that COVID-19 is not that monster. Only everyone has to be careful. All friends and family should be connected with each other through calls and video calls. Normal colds and coughs cannot always be an infection of this virus.

Now the doctor and his family were friends of Roohi and Anu. They no longer felt alone.

"Anu dear, thank you so much you've done a lot for me. Dr Dhananjaya saved my life but you supported me and understood my situation and only a real friend can do this" Roohi embraced Anu while saying.

Anu was eager to know what was that Dhananjaya brought out of Roohi's head. What was it that remained concealed throughout a long friendship of three years with Roohi? She felt uneasy then after thinking for a few minutes she phoned Dr Dhananjaya.

"Sir. This is Anu...first, thanks again for helping us. sir, secondly. Please don't mind my asking what was it that made Roohi sick? What was it that I could not understand after being so close to her? Sir. This thing is eating me. if you could tell me. " Anu hardly managed to speak.

"Any. This is my profession to help people with these issues. Yes, something was there that she hid from you from the very beginning of your friendship, I guess. Roohi was not the only child to her parents...she had a brother who suffered from Pneumonia when Roohi was eight. Say at a very tender age. Her brother could not be recovered from this disease and they lost him. From that day onward Roohi became very sensitive regarding any kind of illness. Roohi's parents are working. They could not yield enough time to Roohi and she nurtured a fear of losing life under certain circumstances in her subconscious mind... that's it. I just made her talk a lot and brought out the chief reason..." Dhananjaya uttered to Anu's surprise.

"Ooh...it was the story. Sir. But it's good that now she has recovered completely..." Anu took a long breath of ease.

HOMECOMING

HOMECOMING

-Dr Arvind Mishra

(Translated from Hindi by Kshama Gautam)

A Scientist, a Science Fictionist, a critic and an editor, Dr Arvind Mishra is a credentialed researcher in multiple streams of Science and Science Fiction with several published books, and more than one thousand published articles, essays and stories across various magazines, newspapers and more. He is an active blogger on popular Science and Science Fiction internet media and has delivered Radio and Television shows on the same subjects. Dr Mishra is a decorated member of several Indian and International Science Fiction communities and organisations.

The whole world was gradually getting back to normal living from the Covid 19 pandemic caused by a hitherto unknown respiratory coronavirus. It had been ten years since this epidemic which spread from a Wuhan city wet market of China in December 2019, had engulfed the entire world. There was a great loss whether it was people or wealth. The entire world had turned dilapidated and lifeless. By the end of the year 2020, mankind was attacked by the second wave of this epidemic which was even more violent and infectious than the first. When it subsided in 2021 after ending the lives of millions of people all over the world, a lot of countries had been economically ruined. In many countries, poor people starved for bread. But with time, people became accustomed to staying with it. People came closer to one another emotionally but the physical distance sustained. They would greet one another from far away, maintaining a certain distance. There were faces hidden by masks. To avoid any identity crisis, a large-size photo of the face was hung on the chest of volunteers and corona warriors. The infection rate of the epidemic had dwindled but the virus could not be completely eradicated. At times, there was news of its spread suddenly from some part of the world but it was quickly curbed. Like the AIDS virus, this virus has also become man's forever companion. It was a foe in disguise.

******

Ten years passed by in no time. There was a lot of discussion about a book on Amazon's online marketing website containing the details of the famous people of the world who survived this ordeal. Names of many industrialists and political personalities were also mentioned including the Prime Ministers of Britain and Russia. Popular personalities of Hollywood and Bollywood could also be seen there. In this, one entry was of Tanmay Kumar, an industrialist, who was born in India and settled in America. He survived the pandemic but returned to India due to the bankruptcy of his multinational company. He returned to India and was spending a life of anonymity. Some said that he ran a charity in Bangalore, while others were of the statement that he was seen among the sages at Ganga Ghat in Banaras. Such was the havoc Corona wreaked on people. Indian readers would often click on the Indian entries in this Amazon Kindle edition of the book, in which Tanmay Kumar's story featured prominently. And then they would start reading it...

*****

The name of Indian-origin American Tanmay Kumar was included among the ten trillionaires of the world. Tanmay, a native of Bangalore, had created a stir with his innovations in the IT and AI sectors. By patenting his artificial intelligence and virtual reality new devices and selling them to multinational companies, he had amassed so much wealth that even his next ten descendants and relatives could be brought up without doing anything. And it was obvious that such a prodigious talent had to reach America sooner or later. Consequently, he formed a multinational company on his own in America named 'Indiatech AI Solutions.' Tanmay Kumar was known not only for his wealth but also for his generosity and philanthropic activities. He donated freely for the promotion of modern education in many cities of India. He also had the unique quality of predicting the future.

He had already predicted so many upcoming technologies.

One of his much-discussed predictions, which he predicted around 2001, was the spread of a global pandemic. Just like the Spanish flu-like pandemic that engulfed the entire world during 1918–19. Tanmay Kumar's concern was that the world had not taken his warning seriously in time. America itself had not paid any attention to his prediction. It is said that his warning remained buried in some classified files of the White House. Presidents had come and gone but that file could not be opened and gathered dust only. And then as an unfortunate coincidence exactly after 100 years of Spanish flu, the great misery in the world in 2020 arrived and turned into a global pandemic caused by a novel type of coronavirus. China was held responsible for the origin of this virus. The series of accusations and counteraccusations took place between America and China in such a way that it seemed as if it would crop up the Third World War. However, the situation at that time left no country in a position to wage a world war. The disaster was caused by the new Corona had made every country economically feeble. A total of three lakh people declared and many undeclared, had died in America itself. This epidemic, which began in March 2020, reached its peak by July. But in the coming spring of 2021, another more intense phase of this disease started due to which about two million people all over the world had lost their lives.

******

Corona was wreaking devastation in America. An atmosphere of such uncertainty had developed that mutual trust had eroded between the White House and the health units battling this epidemic. The Corona meter was rising high. The rate of spread of infection of the virus SARS CoV 2 was not falling below 'R3'. That was, the process of three persons getting infected by one, and then another three spread it to make even a large number and thus it continued to increase geometrically. If this rate of spread of infection had persisted, then the death toll in America would have taken about five lakh people in just a month. Deaths were happening in other countries of the world too, but they were around R2. In India this rate was R1.5. There, strict compliance with the timely lockdown had kept the rate of infection in check. But the freedom-loving people in America had bought themselves great misery. There the infection had reached small towns and villages. The supply chain of essential commodities was snapped. There was an atmosphere of chaos all around. Everyone was panicked.

*****

This was the time when Tanmay Kumar got engrossed in public service like an angel. Taking necessary safety precautions for himself, he got busy arranging the supply of essential goods along with the team of self-sacrificing young volunteers from remote villages in America. One day, before leaving for this campaign, he called his advocate Edward Ruth.

Edward Ruth arrived on time. Tanmay Kumar was ready to go for the social service campaign. He explained to him the risks associated with his mission and handed him an envelope with instructions to open it only if he fell into a prolonged unconsciousness or coma or died because of the pandemic. Edward Ruth understood that this would be his client's will. After this brief meeting, Tanmay Kumar left on his campaign. He was monitoring activities like providing essential commodities to people confined to their homes due to the fear of Corona and disposal of dead bodies of elderly people, quarantined in some homes and lost their lives because of the pandemic. The calamity was so great that at times he considered himself defeated. But he was so devoted to social service that he could not stop himself.

His determination pushed him ahead. Meanwhile, some young members of his team were caught by the pandemic. It was fortunate that due to his strong immunity, he carried out his campaign during the intense period of the epidemic and remained unaffected by Corona. His entire team was busy with its work every day. Then one day the untoward incident happened. Tanmay Kumar's self-alert device informed him that he was infected with a potent new Coronavirus mutant. His medical team had warned him that he had an overactive immune system, a condition known medically as an immune disorder, which can sometimes be life-threatening. He was immediately admitted to the hospital designated for the COVID-19 pandemic. Along with his doctors, a whole team of Covid experts got involved in his examination. A sample was taken from his trachea. Now he was under the supervision of skilled doctors every moment.

*****

A meeting was in progress between Tanmay Kumar's doctors and the doctors of the designated Corona Hospital regarding his health. The matter of great importance in their discussion was the fact that if his overactive immune system reacts abnormally to the new coronavirus, could it be fatal? “And then this immune disorder response will become deadly,” said his doctor.

"Yes, it may result in what is called ‘cytokine storm’, that is, his lungs and other vital organs of the body will also become nonfunctional, and then it will be difficult to save him from multiple organ failure. New corona-infected patients are not able to be saved even on a ventilator in this situation." Said the chief physician of Corona Hospital.

"Why don't we talk to Tanmay Kumar about this situation and clarify the situation to him?" He added. His physician found this opinion appropriate. And he thought it best to talk to Tanmay Kumar about this.

Tanmay Kumar was listening seriously to the words of his physician Dr. Christopher. At this stage, the coronavirus infection was limited to his upper respiratory tract, but it would not take long for it to reach the lungs. Till now the symptoms were limited to mild fever and headache. There was just a slight soreness in the throat. On video call, he became engrossed in listening to the suggestions of Dr. Christopher and other doctors.

"Are you all of the same opinion that my super active immunity can be fatal for me?" he uttered in a feeble voice.

"Yes," there was collective consensus among the doctors.

"How long do you think it will take to reach that level?" There was a tremor in Tanmay Kumar's voice. "Two or three days." The physicians replied.

"What is the possibility of survival in such a situation?" Tanmay Kumar asked in a calm, controlled but curious voice.

"There is no conventional treatment for the new coronavirus as of now and your case is different. You have a known history of an immune disorder. We cannot let the case deteriorate to that point." Dr. Christopher clarified.

"This means that my death is inevitable." This time there was a notable inconsistency in Tanmay Kumar's voice.

"An entire team of doctors is dedicated to saving your life, but we are helpless vis a vis this new coronavirus. It is a sneaky virus. Its behavior also varies from patient to patient having different immunities. Since you are a victim of hypersensitive immunity, we are taking extra precautions, however... "

Tanmay Kumar interrupted his doctor,

"However, what?"

"We.... we have limits sir; we are not almighty."

" Okay, okay, is there any solution or any treatment?"

"Not in the current medical science, yes, work is being done on many medicinal formulations and vaccines for the treatment of this epidemic, maybe some way will be found soon…"

*****

The moment came when a cytokine storm started in Tanmay Kumar's lungs and since no treatment was possible to stop it, the doctors unanimously put him in a cryogenic capsule. This left him in a state of suspended animation. This was to remain as such until an effective immune suppressor was discovered to stop the cytokine storm. Time was passing by.

*****

Tanmay Kumar's company, Indiatech IT Solutions invited scientists to develop immunity suppressor drugs with a huge prize money award. After the Covid 19 pandemic, the international business of immunity booster medicines – herbal medicine and Ayurvedic remedies had reached several billion dollars, in which India alone had a 40 per cent share. Indian pharmaceutical trade got a big boost due to the decline in China's credibility at the international level. Various types of immunity booster formulae were being sold at a rapid pace - people were now very conscious about avoiding germs. But no one had thought about immunity suppressors. After all, how many people were there with hyperimmunity? Not even one per cent of the world's population whose immune system becomes overactive to any germ and becomes fatal for themselves. To date, there is no effective medicine for such immunity disorder diseases in modern medicine. So many people like Tanmay Kumar were cursed to live with this unusual ability. There were plenty of immunity boosters but there was not even a single immunity suppressor to date. The appeal of Tanmay Kumar's company had an impact. And scientists worked day and night to invent an effective immunity suppressor.

*****

Many pharmaceutical companies of the world were engaged in manufacturing immunity suppressors, but the success was achieved by the 'Day Labs' of Bangalore. The drug was found to be effective in animal, clinical and control trials. Tanmay Kumar's company bought the manufacturing rights of this medicine. Complete five years had passed. The doctors decided to try the medicine by taking Tanmay Kumar out of the cryonic capsule. An entire medical team was monitoring the effect of this medicine very closely. Liberating him from the cryonic capsule, and bringing the body to normal temperature, other life-saving drugs and immunity suppressor drugs were used simultaneously. It had a miraculous effect. Tanmay Kumar's lungs were saved from the cytokine storm. Meaning, that his hyperactive immune system died off which would otherwise have been fatal. The lungs were spared from excessive mucus secretion. Then the deadly effect of coronavirus also disappeared. Other antiviral medicines had also come into use by now. Due to this Tanmay Kumar moved towards speedy recovery. He was discharged from the hospital after necessary quarantine.

*****

In these five years, the world of information technology has transformed. The innovations in artificial intelligence that Tanmay Kumar had created were now outdated. His business was on the verge of shutting down. Now, mind-to-mind communication and the ability to read thoughts have come into existence. It was the era of modern gadgets of virtual head bearers, holographic image projections and webinars. Tanmay Kumar soon realized that he was no longer going to survive in the market. The Covid pandemic had left him nowhere. The company with billions in turnover was now heading towards bankruptcy. Tanmay Kumar's heart was completely distracted from worldly matters. The desire to return to his homeland began to intensify in his heart. One day he called his advocate and canceled his previous will. The company was closed after paying the employees their dues and san adequate amount of living expenses from their savings. He returned to his homeland

www.ingramcontent.com/pod-product-compliance
Lightning Source LLC
LaVergne TN
LVHW041914070526
838199LV00051BA/2617